أيـــان جمـيـــلة

Ayat Jamilah:
Beautiful Signs

أيـات جمـيلة

Ayat Jamilah:

Beautiful Signs

A TREASURY OF ISLAMIC WISDOM FOR CHILDREN AND PARENTS

collected and adapted by **Sarah Conover and Freda Crane**

Illustrations by **Valerie Wahl**

This Little Light of Mine Series

Kindness: A Treasury of Buddhist Wisdom for Children and Parents

Ayat Jamilah: Beautiful Signs: A Treasury of Islamic Wisdom for Children and Parents

Eastern Washington University Press · Spokane, Washington · 2004

Library of Congress Cataloging-in-Publication Data

Conover, Sarah.
    Ayat jamilah = Beautiful signs : a treasury of Islamic wisdom for children and parents / by Sarah Conover and Freda Crane.-- 1st ed.
        p. cm. -- (Little light of mine series)
Includes bibliographical references.
    ISBN 0-910055-94-7 (pbk. : alk. paper)
        1. Islamic stories--Juvenile literature. 2. Islam--Quotations, maxims, etc.--Juvenile literature. [1. Islamic stories.] 1. Title: Beautiful signs. II. Crane, Freda. III. Title. IV. Series.
    BP87.5.C66 2003
    297.1'8--dc22
                        2003023954

For my beloved, Doug. Your love, generosity, humor and wisdom make me a believer.

Sarah Conover

For my husband, Mohammed Shamma, my guide and companion on the spiritual path and on the path to diversity within a world community. And to my grandchildren for whom the book is written: Samiya, Bayann and Yousef Shamma; and Ayah Jamilah and Zahra Firdous Syeed.

Freda Crane

Contents

We showed them Sign after Sign each
Greater than its fellow.

Of Allah's Signs, one is that He created you
from dust; and lo,
you become human beings ranging far and wide.

And among God's Signs,
Another is ... that He engenders love
And tenderness between you,
Planted love and kindness in your hearts ...

And yet others of Allah's Signs
Are the creation of the heavens and the earth,
And the differences of your languages and complexions ...

And yet among Allah's Signs,
He shows you the lightning,
... He sends down rain from the sky
and with it gives life to the earth ...

Verily in this are
Signs for those who reflect.

Qur'an 43:48; 30:20–25

Preface

In *Ayat Jamilah: Beautiful Signs,* we have done our best to provide the reader with stories that draw from the diverse reaches of Islamic culture across distance and time—from China in the north to Tanzania in the south, from Morocco in the west to Indonesia in the east, from the time of the Prophet Muhammad ﷺ[1] in the 7th century CE[2] through the millennium and a half of his influence. By presenting this assortment, we hope to unhinge the fixed notion that links camels to Muslims. Many of the world's most significant historical eras and diverse cultures are but beads on Islam's lengthy necklace. Only the very first Muslims, living in the Arabian Peninsula, constituted a unity of Islamic culture.

The word "Islam" means peace and submission to God. The followers of Islam are Muslims, according to Arabic grammar, which adds a 'M' to the beginning of a word to denote a person doing that action.

The Qur'an, the holy book of Islam, and hadiths, words and actions of the Prophet, form the common thread of Islamic spirituality and ethics on which the stories in this treasury are based. We have included four general types: stories from the Qur'an, the divine revelations given to the Prophet Muhammad; stories from the collections of hadiths; stories of historical Muslims; and lastly, folk tales. The stories considered true portray incidents about the Prophet, those close to him, and other exemplary figures in the Islamic narrative. The tales are clearly

---

[1] This symbol is the Arabic phrase for "God's peace be upon him", which is used whenever someone is speaking of Prophet Muhammad.

[2] Abbreviation for Common Era.

introduced as such, with a legend-like introduction, and, if from the Middle East, with the Arabic equivalent to "once upon a time" — kan ya ma kan, there was and there was not ...

In creating this treasury, Dr. Crane and I have had the great pleasure of delving into the ancient texts, Holy Scriptures, mystical verse, and imaginative tales of Islam. We've had the opportunity to compare translations, comb through our individual, assorted material collected over some years, sort, discuss and choose our favorite characters and stories.

You'll find the famous Joha, one and the same as Hodja, Goha or Mulla Nasruddin—the funny and wise Muslim pundit—whether he turns up in China or Egypt. We've included some of Islam's most important women: from Khadija, the first wife of the Prophet, who offered him unconditional support, to Rabiah of Basra, one of Islam's earliest Sufis.[3] Wanting our audience to experience the direct-link to Islam's cousins, Judaism and Christianity, we've included stories about Ibrahim (Abraham), Isa (Jesus), and Mariam (Mary), Jesus' mother, which are found in Muslim sources.

In compiling these stories and sayings we hope to reach several different audiences. First, our goal is that this book be meaningful and broadening to parents and children of diverse faiths interested in learning from one of the world's great wisdom traditions. Second, this anthology is intended to be a resource for the educator trying to convey more than a textbook sense of Islam to students studying geography, world history, and world religions. Finally, it is written with the aim that Muslim families may find in it some of the most important stories of their faith, as well as some surprises from the far corners of the Muslim world.

Dr. Crane and I came to this book project with significant similarities as well as differences.

[3] A Sufi is a Muslim who has given up interest in the material world in favor of seeking closer contact with Allah, God.

We both are educators; we both have collected Muslim stories for young adults; we both have an enormous appreciation for the inspired story-telling of the Muslim world; and finally, we both perceive a need for this book. I am not Muslim, Dr. Crane is. We wanted a book that would have one foothold in the secular-educational world, and one foot firmly planted in the religion. As a team, our goal is that this book be a bridge between the two domains.

There was, and is still, a lack of compelling material introducing Islam to children and young adults. I studied Islam as a comparative religions major in college, but it was after having children of my own, over a decade ago, that I felt the need for a book like this. Later, as a high school teacher, I found myself again looking for stories, poems and sayings that could convey more than a sterile sampling of Islamic ethics and spirituality. Dr. Crane, as the children's book reviewer for the Islamic Society of North America, had long perceived the need for this book too, collecting stories with this project in mind for thirty years. We are both very grateful to have found each other.

Today's high-stakes political climate, tinged with religious conflict, has made the need for accessible introductory material on Islam more vivid. Our true hope is that this book will be a modest, but useful contribution towards redressing that shortfall.

—Sarah Conover

To the Reader

 [1]"There is no doubt about it. Something has to be done about this man," said one of the merchants. "Not only is he telling people that there is only one God whom they should worship, but he is gaining followers from all the different tribes in Mecca. If he keeps on like this, people might stop coming here every year."

It was the year 615 CE in the city of Mecca, in the desert of the Arabian Peninsula, five years after Muhammad ﷺ received his first revelation from God. For many years now, the Ka'bah, the holy shrine in the center of the city, had held various idols, attracting worshippers who made the pilgrimage each year to Mecca. The money they brought with them was good for business.

"It won't be easy to stop Muhammad," said one of Mecca's leaders. "Muhammad has allies in every tribe. We can't harm him because he is a member of the Quraish tribe, the most powerful tribe of Arabia."

Finally Utba, one of the Quraish chiefs, came up with a solution. That very day he went to see Muhammad, to try to convince him to stop talking about the One God, Allah.[2]

---

[1] This Arabic calligraphy says, "In the name of Allah, Most Gracious, and Most Merciful." Each story will begin with this saying, done in a variety of calligraphic styles. It is customary for Muslims to begin any good action, such as eating, with this phrase.

[2] Allah is the Arabic word for God, so in this book the words Allah and God will be used interchangeably.

"O Muhammad, you are one of us. As you know, we are the noblest of the tribes, with a worthy ancestry. Listen to me and I will make some suggestions, and perhaps you will be able to accept one of them." Muhammad agreed to listen, so Utba continued. "If what you want is wealth, we will contribute from our own property until you are the wealthiest man in Mecca.

"If what you want is honor and power, we will make you our chief and give you such power that nothing can be done without your consent. Even if you want to be a king, we will not hesitate to crown you king over us. If you are unable to cure yourself of the visions that you have been seeing, we will find a physician for you and do everything in our power to get you cured."

How could anyone decline such an offer? All that Muhammad had to do in return for these rewards was agree that all gods were equal.

After listening patiently to Utba, Muhammad spoke. "Now please listen to me," he said and then quoted this verse from the Qur'an, which had been revealed to him some time before:

This is revealed by Allah, the Compassionate, the Merciful,
A giver of good news and advice:
O Prophet, say: I am but a man like yourselves. It is
revealed to me that your God is One God, therefore
go towards Him and ask His forgiveness.

He refused to stop preaching Islam and a long period of harassment and persecution followed. Because the Prophet Muhammad was from a powerful clan, no one felt free to harm him personally, but some of the new Muslims were slaves or immigrants without anyone to protect them.

The black slave, Bilal, for instance, was left in the burning desert sun without food or drink, held down by a large boulder. Bilal's owner came by every few hours to ask him to denounce the message of Muhammad. While he could still speak, he would say, "There is only one God." When he could no longer speak, he would lift a finger on his right hand, to indicate One God. He was saved from death only because Abu Bakr, a wealthy Muslim, happened to see Bilal and bought him his freedom.

Although this was a very difficult period for the new Muslims, the Prophet Muhammad acted with patience and kindness. As a deliberate insult, one neighboring woman would empty her garbage in front of Muhammad's house each day, and verbally insult him at every chance. When Muhammad didn't see her for two days and there was no garbage on his doorstep, he asked someone about her. Muhammad was told that she had fallen sick, so he immediately went to visit, to ask what he could do to help her.

Finally, after thirteen years of torture and discrimination, Muhammad told the Muslims they should move to the city of Madinah where they could be safe. This migration (*Hijrah* in Arabic), from Mecca to Madinah, marks the beginning of the Islamic calendar, the year 1 AH (After Hijrah). It was also the beginning of the Muslim community: after this move, so many people became Muslim that Muhammad became the political leader as well as the spiritual leader of most of Arabia. He could have chosen to be wealthy, but the Prophet distributed all he had to those in need, and continued to live very simply.

One time he and his friend, Abu Hurayrah, went to the market to buy some clothes. The seller stood up and tried to kiss the Prophet's hand. Muhammad quickly withdrew his hand to stop the man from kissing it and told him, "This is the practice of the Persians with their kings. I am not a king. I am only a man like you."

Having a prophet of God living among them offered Muslims the opportunity to see how one could put Allah's words into action. Sometimes when Muhammad led the community in prayer, his grandchildren would climb on his back to play while he knelt with his forehead touching the ground. He would wait a little so they could play and get down easily before he stood to continue prayer. Once, when Muhammad kissed his grandson, a man nearby said, "I have ten children and I have never kissed any of them."

The Prophet Muhammad looked at him sadly and answered, "Whoever is not merciful to others will not be treated mercifully."

He also told many wise stories. Once he told the story of a man in the desert who was very thirsty. Finally the man found a well of water, but there was no bucket to bring the water up, so he climbed down in the well to drink. After a difficult climb back up he saw a dog panting and eating mud because of excessive thirst. The man thought to himself, this dog is suffering from the same problem as I. So he went back down in the well, filled his shoe with water, held it with his teeth so he could climb back up and gave it to the dog. People asked the Prophet, "Is there a reward for us in serving animals?" He replied, "Yes, there is a reward for serving anything alive."

The Prophet Muhammad lived until the age of 63, and died content that the message of Allah was spreading beyond the desert to the world. He had established Islam not only as a religion, but as a system of law, and a lifestyle which fundamentally changed the society around him.

✽✽✽✽✽✽✽✽✽✽✽✽✽✽✽✽

Although Prophet Muhammad ﷺ lived over 1400 years ago, Muslims still follow his actions, words, and the revelations he received from God. The actions and words of Muhammad himself are collected in books of hadiths. Muslims are very careful not to make up stories about the Prophet, and every hadith has been carefully researched to make sure it was conveyed by reliable people.

The words that God spoke to Muhammad through the voice of the Angel Gabriel are written in The Holy Qur'an. The Qur'an is a book of guidance and good ethics. With each piece of advice comes the reminder that Allah knows all, and is the best judge of a person's deeds. "The Qur'an guides to the straight path and gives glad tidings of a great reward to the believers who do good works."

The book you are now reading is a collection of stories and sayings treasured in different regions of the Muslim world. The stories and wisdom taken from the Qur'an and hadiths are known to Muslims everywhere.

Some of the other stories are known only in one area, and some, like those of the character known as the Honorable Joha, or Mulla Nasruddin or Nasruddin Hodja, are known in many places, but have slight differences because the folk figure is considered born in that particular area. I have enjoyed Joha stories for so many years, that I now consider him part of my family.

I hope all these stories will help you appreciate that although we may vary in our outward appearance and customs, our humanity is but one.

—Freda Crane

Stories and Sayings

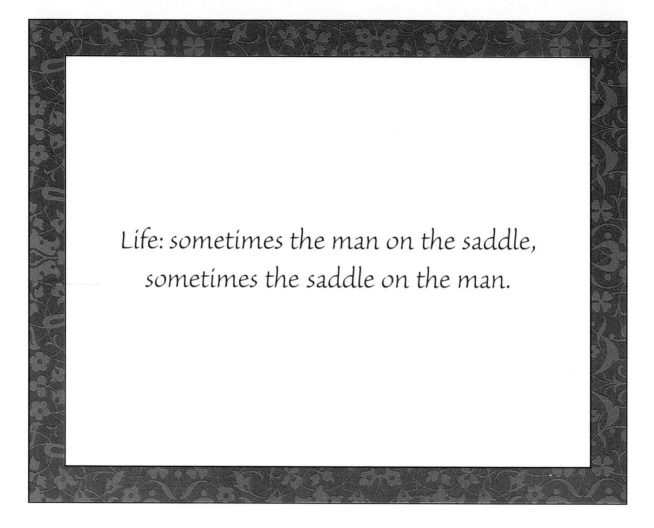

Life: sometimes the man on the saddle, sometimes the saddle on the man.

The Honorable Joha, Mulla Nasruddin Hodja and the Famous Donkey Story

 Kan ya ma kan: there was and there was not a time when Joha and his son set out for the market with their donkey walking along behind them. They passed several men sitting outside a shop drinking tea and heard some of their remarks.

"Look at that man! How can he be so mean as to make his child walk all the way to the market when he has a donkey the child could easily ride?"

Joha immediately picked up his son and put him on the donkey's back. They continued this way for awhile, until they passed several women who were also on their way to the market.

"For shame," said one woman to another. "Look at that child, riding the donkey while he makes his father walk. Doesn't he have any respect for his elders?"

Right away, Joha took his son off the donkey, and got on himself. They had traveled only slightly farther, when someone else criticized the father for being so selfish—riding on the donkey while making his son walk. In response to this criticism, Joha picked up the child and placed him on the saddle directly in front of him.

Alas this maneuver also brought forth criticism. "How mean they are to overload the donkey like that!" cried an old man to his friend.

There is only one thing to do, thought Joha in despair. He and his son dismounted. After a great deal of effort, Joha managed to heave the donkey upon his own back. Only a little way down the road, everyone was laughing at the stupid man carrying his donkey instead of riding it.

Shamefaced, Joha put down the donkey, and they continued to the market exactly as they had started—with all three walking. Some minutes later, Joha looked at his son: "So you see," he said with a wise nod, "it is clearly not possible to please all people. It is better to do what you know is right and please God."

While you still have the power
of speech use it in gladness and joy!
Tomorrow, when the Angel
of Death appears you will have
no choice other than silence.

The Bandage: A True Story of Rabiah Al Adawiya of Basra

 One day, Rabiah of Basra came upon a man with a sorrowful face, his head bound by an immense white bandage. Stopping the man, Rabiah made some inquiries.

"Sir," she asked him, "What's this bandage about? Are you wounded?"

"Not really," he replied. "But I have a painful headache."

Rabiah looked puzzled. "How old are you?" she asked further.

"I'm thirty years old," said the man.

"And have you enjoyed good health for most of those years?"

"*Al hamdu lil Allah*, thanks be to God," he replied, "I have had good health my whole life."

He smiled weakly, "But I have a terrible headache now!"

Rabiah pondered his words for some moments. "For thirty years," she said at last, "God has granted you excellent health, but you never once bound yourself with a bandage of gratitude! Yet now, bothered by a small ache, you have wrapped your head in a showy complaint to Allah."

The man knew she had spoken wisely, and said nothing in his defense. But he was afterwards known, for the rest of his long life, as the man who never, ever complained.

God brings forth the living
from the dead,
and brings forth the dead
from the living;
and God enlivens the earth
after its death:
and *so* will you all be brought forth.

The Brothers: A Hausa Tale from West Africa

 Once there was and twice there wasn't two old brothers who were inseparable travelers: one was named Life, the other Death. One time, after journeying across a desert, they came to a refreshing green oasis where they were greeted by the spring-keeper.

"Would you like some cool water to drink?" he asked them. Both the men nodded their assent. Dipping his gourd into the pool, the spring-keeper added, "It is the custom to let the elder drink first. Which one of you is the elder?"

Life spoke up first. "I am the elder," he said, stepping forward.

"No," Death contradicted, "I am the elder." And he stepped forward too, next to his brother.

Life smiled, but said, "That is impossible. Things must live before they die."

Death responded, "On the contrary, things begin in death, are born, live for a time and then return to death."

Said Life, "That's not how it works at all. All things come from the Creator, live and then die. Death began after the first creature lived and died."

Said Death, a spark in his eyes: "Death is the before and after of all life. Things arise from it and return to it; therefore, death is the elder."

The two debated like this next to the spring, and had yet to drink a drop of water. Finally, they asked the spring-keeper to judge truly who the eldest was.

"Gentleman, I cannot say," said the spring-keeper. "What you've each told me is true." He looked at the two brothers. "How can one speak of death without life? Death is like a desert until rain falls; then, all the living things sprout miraculously from the rocks and sand." He smiled. "And how can one speak of life without death, to which all things are certain to return?" The spring-keeper paused. "Neither can exist without the other: the Creator wears both these two masks. Neither of you is elder or younger."

He held out a single gourd. "Drink now, together, and go in peace."

And the two travelers took the gourd, drank their fill, and headed off in the comfort of each other's company.

There is no compulsion in religion.
True direction is in fact
distinct from error:
so whoever disbelieves in idols and
believes in God has taken hold
of the most reliable handle
which does not break.

It's Not the Sun: From the Qur'an

Ibrahim (Abraham), grew up in Mesopotamia during the time when people worshipped many gods. Watching his relatives fashion them from wood, he often wondered how they could worship the statues they themselves had made. Finally, one day he decided to begin his own search for God.

The day passed without Ibrahim making any progress. When night fell, he saw a shining star, and thought: *this star is so bright—this is surely my God.* But when the star set and he could no longer see it, he said: "I cannot love stars that set." He knew that a real God would not disappear.

When he saw the moon rising in splendor, he thought: *this is my God!* But when the moon set, he said again, "I cannot love something which sets. Unless the true God guides me, I will certainly be misled."

Bismillah Al Rahman Al Rahim, in the name of God, Most Gracious, Most Merciful.

When he saw the sun rising in full brilliance he said: "This must be my God, for this is the greatest of all." When the sun set, however, Ibrahim realized that Allah must be above all things and greater than any of His creations.

God chose Ibrahim to become a prophet and commanded him to call his people to the truth. Ibrahim shared Allah's message with the people, but no one cared to follow his guidance.

One day, the people of the town went out for a picnic. When they returned, they discovered most of their idols broken on the ground. Only the largest one still stood, now with an axe hanging around his neck. They cried out, "Who has done this to our gods?"

"I heard Ibrahim talk against our idols. Maybe he did it," suggested someone. So they brought Ibrahim in front of the people.

"Are you the one who did this to our gods, Ibrahim?" they asked him.

Ibrahim pointed to a statue and answered, "Why don't you ask the biggest one? See, he has a hammer there next to him. Ask him!"

"You know full well that these idols don't speak and they cannot move!" the people replied angrily.

Ibrahim answered, "Then why do you insist on worshipping something that can't see or think or even defend itself?"

The people of course had no answer for this, and yet they continued in their old ways. Being a prophet of great wisdom and patience, Ibrahim continued to deliver his message until his Lord sent him elsewhere.

The human race is created
from the one source.
If one man feels pain, the others,
from the same source,
cannot be indifferent to it.

Manifold Increase: A True Story of Uthman ibn Affan

 The sparse rain that comes but once or twice a year to much of the desert means the difference between bounty and famine. In the year 640 CE, the rain did not come to Arabia at all; the crops failed and the people faced starvation. Tribes of bedouins flocked to Madinah seeking help. Everyone's survival depended on the timely arrival of food carried by caravan over the wide expanse of sand to the city.

The sound of a galloping horse was welcome noise to the townspeople who knew it signaled that a caravan was in the vicinity. And indeed a scout rode in to announce the approach of Uthman ibn Affan's caravan of 1000 camels loaded with food.

With food so scarce, the owner of the caravan could name any price for the goods it carried. The other merchants hurried to meet with Uthman, hoping to buy at least part of the cargo.

Even if they paid three times what Uthman had paid, they could still get rich by reselling at higher prices to desperately hungry people.

The merchants were disappointed, but not too surprised, when Uthman refused to sell, saying that he had received a better offer. Since he was the most successful merchant in the area, they had expected him to drive a hard bargain.

The next strategy the merchants tried was to join together in order to match or better the other offer Uthman had received. But no matter what they suggested, even *five* times the price he had paid for the food, Uthman still maintained that he had received a better offer. The merchants puzzled over this: who was better able to buy than they, and what was this price they could not match?

One of them asked, "Who has made you this offer, and what exactly is it?"

Uthman smiled. "It is Allah, who promises me many times the value of my goods if I give them away for His sake."

The merchants bowed their heads in shame, remembering that the Qur'an states: "Those who spend their wealth in the way of God are like a grain of corn. It grows seven ears and each ear has a hundred grains."

The next morning Uthman's caravan was unloaded in the middle of the market. His agent called out to the public:

> Come one, come all,
> this food is free;
> a gift from Allah
> to those in need.

"How can one obtain wisdom?"
asked a boy.
Mulla Nasruddin replied,
"Always listen attentively to what
the wise and learned men tell you.
And if you are speaking to others,
listen carefully to what you are saying."

The Honorable Joha, Mulla Nasruddin Hodja and the Tricky Case

Long, long ago, a poor widow came to Mulla Nasruddin's court for advice one day. Having written her name on the list of petitioners, she stood to the side and waited her turn.

At last her name was hailed and she humbly stepped before the Mulla. "Your Honor," she began, "I am poor, with no husband to help me raise my son. My child has an addiction to sugar, of which I cannot cure him. Although we have barely enough to eat, there seems to be nothing I can do or say to keep him from squandering our few coins on sweets. I am here to ask if the Court might forbid him to eat any."

Mulla Nasruddin stroked his beard, his gaze serious as he contemplated the widow's request. "The Court must give this problem thorough consideration," replied the Mulla. "Please come back in a week's time and, *inshaa Allah*, God willing, we will have a judgment for you."

A week later, the widow again placed her name upon the list of petitioners and waited her turn. She led her son to the head of the court when her name was called. "I am ready for your pronouncement, Your Honor, and I have brought my son so that he may hear it from your own lips."

Mulla Nasruddin looked at mother and son and slowly shook his head from side to side. "I am truly sorry," said the Mulla. "This is a difficult case. The Court must postpone the pronouncement for another week."

A bit confused, but still hopeful, the widow returned home with her son.

A week later, and then the week after that, the widow met with the same response from the Mulla. But she persisted. A month after her first visit to the Mulla, the widow stood before him, anxiously clasping the hand of her son. "And so," the widow asked, "Do you have an order for my son?"

The Mulla shifted forward in his chair, leaned towards the boy and fixed his eyes on him. "Boy!" shouted the Mulla, "By the authority of this court, you are hereby forbidden to more than a half ounce of sugar a day!"

The boy cowered. Beaming, the widow knew her problem was solved. She thanked the Mulla for his help, and began to walk away with her son. But then she stopped, turned to face the Mulla again, and asked that he might answer just one more question.

"Mulla," she said, "Why did you not make that pronouncement weeks ago, when I first came to you? Why did you wait so many weeks?"

Mulla Nasruddin looked surprised. "I had to cure myself of the same habit, didn't I? How could I have known it would take so long?"

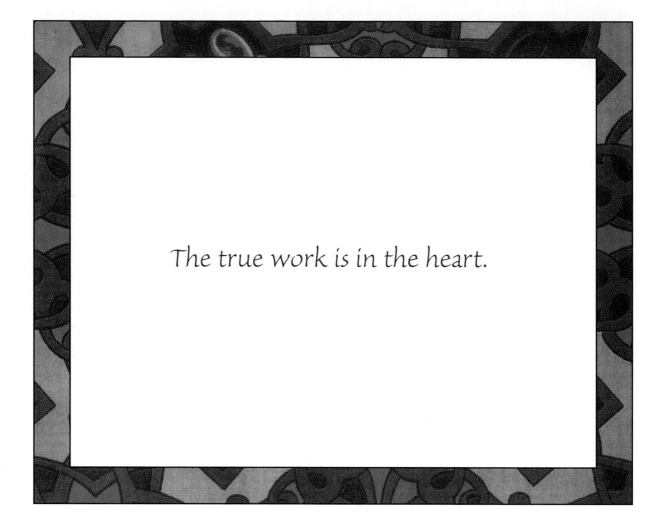

The true work is in the heart.

The Wise Sailimai: a Tale from China

 Long, long ago in the country of China, lived a young woman of the Muslim Hui people named Sailimai. Although she was a farm girl, too poor to attend school, Sailimai nonetheless paid close attention to life around her. When an old woman in the village needed help—but was too proud to ask for it—Sailimai would know just the right time to visit. When children scraped their knees, Sailimai arrived to assist, even if they were not her own children. She may have been poor and unschooled, but Sailimai possessed a wise and deep heart.

Once, her father-in-law, a carpenter named Ali, was ordered by the emperor to make some repairs in his palace. Fearful of doing less than his best for the emperor, Ali pushed himself to work his very hardest, working both day and night. Yet, as it sometimes happens, the time came when Ali went beyond his limits. Dizzy with fatigue, hands shaking, momentarily careless, Ali tipped over the emperor's most precious vase. The pieces shattered—all too loudly—in the great hall. Servants came running.

Soon enough the emperor heard the story of his ruined, priceless vase.

"Bring this carpenter to me at once," he demanded.

Handcuffed and escorted by three guards, Ali, trembling, stood speechless before the emperor. The emperor drew his sword. As it hovered over Ali's head, Ali at last spoke up: "Forgive me your worship! I did not mean to break the vase. I promise to pay for it. I promise to pay!"

The emperor lowered his sword just a bit. "A poor, old Hui like yourself could never replace such a treasure. Do not jest with me!"

"Have mercy on me," Ali begged. "I will pay."

The emperor re-sheathed his sword with a sly smile. "Very well old Hui. I do not expect you to replace my vase. Instead, I will give you ten days to find me four things." The emperor hesitated in thought, tugging lightly on his beard. "The first thing you must get me is something more black than the bottom of a pan. Second: you must find me something clearer than a mirror." The emperor waited a moment, watching Ali's reaction, but Ali stared blankly at the floor. The emperor continued. "The third: something stronger than steel." The emperor smirked. "And lastly, find me something as vast as the sea. If you fail at any of these, I will chop off your head." Finished, the emperor smiled broadly, quite pleased with himself.

Ali looked stricken. *How,* he wondered, *could I achieve these impossible tasks? Does the emperor simply wish to torture me for the last ten days of my life?* Sick with dread, he hung his head, turned away and headed home.

For the next week he could neither eat nor sleep. His family knew that something was terribly amiss, but Ali would not discuss it. "Please Father," Sailimai said, calling her father-in-law

by the customary term of respect. "What is the trouble? Perhaps we can help." Begging and pleading, Sailimai at last coaxed Ali into talking. He cradled his head between his hands and wept as he named the emperor's four impossible tasks.

But Sailimai responded as if these were everyday requests. "This isn't a problem! Father, don't worry. I will have all these things when the emperor comes tomorrow. I shall present them to him myself!"

Ali assumed that Sailimai was trying only to comfort him. He didn't want her to get in trouble with the emperor too. "Don't be foolish, Sailimai," he warned. These four things do not exist. The emperor just wanted to make me suffer further before killing me."

Sailimai persisted. "Father, I really do have these things. I know you don't believe me now. But wait until tomorrow. I will show them to both you and the emperor!"

And so it was that the very next day, the tenth day since the broken vase, the emperor appeared—surrounded by troops—at Ali's door. "Old Hui! Come forward and give to me the four things you owe me," bellowed the emperor.

Ali came outside with Sailimai by his side. They both bowed humbly, never daring to meet the emperor's gaze. Sailimai then stepped forward. "Your majesty," she said, "The four things you requested are ready to be presented. Please name them one by one."

"The first thing I must have," said the emperor, "is that which is more black than the bottom of a pot." He touched the sheath of his sword with a glint in his eye.

Sailimai answered, "This, your majesty, can be found in a bottomless, greedy heart."

The emperor hid his surprise. *This girl*, he reassured himself, *cannot be so smart. She is a farm girl.* He nodded briefly. "The next thing you must present is something more clear than a mirror. Do you have that?" he asked.

Sailimai answered: "Yes. Knowledge offers a clarity greater than any mirror."

The emperor looked dumbstruck. "Well," he stammered, "Do you have something stronger than steel to give me?"

"Love," said Sailimai, "is the strongest thing in the world."

Knowing he had been bested, the emperor stood speechless. Ali glanced at Sailimai, and stood a little taller. At last the emperor cleared his throat and made his last request. "And what do you have, that could possibly be as vast as the sea?" he asked.

"A virtuous heart is as vast as the sea, your majesty." Her head lowered, Sailimai smiled and said no more.

Flustered and humbled, the emperor sputtered, "It's time to leave. Old Hui, you are hereby pardoned!" He turned to his troops and shouted, "March!"

As the Emperor of China distanced himself, Sailimai held her father-in-law's hand. Together, she and Ali bowed in relief and gratitude to Allah. Because of her wise heart, Ali could now live a long and happy life.

Avoid suspicion as much as possible,
for suspicion in some cases is a sin.
And spy not on each other
nor speak ill of each other
behind your backs.

All in the Family: A Tale from Pakistan

 Once upon a time, all the parts of the body started complaining about the stomach. "It's not fair," they said, "we work all day to give the stomach food, while he does nothing but sit there and enjoy it."

"Well, what can we do about it?" asked the mouth, who was good at saying aloud what others were thinking.

"We can refuse to obey his orders for food," thought the brain, who was good at coming up with solutions. The next day the body parts began their strike.

The brain refused to think about where to look for food.

The feet refused to move towards any food.

The hands refused to pick up anything that might be considered food.

And the ears became deaf to the stomach's rumbling request for something to eat.

All that day and the next, the body parts refused to help the stomach. At first the stomach rested patiently—only an occasional growl of hunger. Soon though, the lack of food began to hurt: the stomach groaned.

"Oh, dear," said the ears. "The stomach sounds like it is really suffering. But it deserves the pain for not helping to gather food." And so the ears ignored the stomach.

The next morning, the stomach twisted in knots from lack of food. The feet didn't care about that, but noticed its own toes cramping. The hands began to lose strength and twitch. The eyes began to weep. The ears rang with weakness, and even the nose started to run.

"Oh my brothers and sisters, my partners in work, I am worried about you," moaned the stomach. "From the food that has come to me I have been feeding you all. I have digested the food and converted it to nutrition for each of you. By means of veins, the food was divided among all of you according to your needs. But alas, now I have no food to send to you and I see that you are all suffering."

Then the other body parts saw the results of their selfishness, and they felt very ashamed. "Please forgive us," pleaded the mouth. "We will not repeat such bad behavior ever again. We see that God has given each of us something different to do, and that if we work together, we will all benefit."

And so the brain thought again
of how to get to the food,
and the feet walked to where it was,
and the eyes showed the hands

where to pick up the food,
and the mouth chewed the food,
and sent it to the stomach
which digested the food
which fed them all.

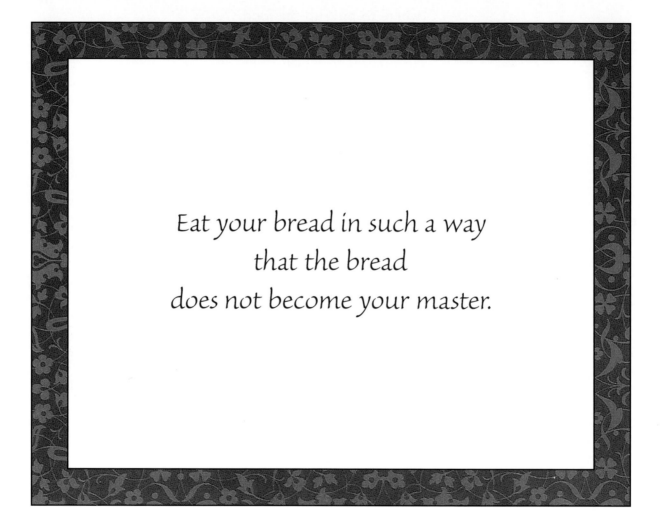

Eat your bread in such a way
that the bread
does not become your master.

What if? A Tale from Iran

Once there was and twice there wasn't a dervish[1] who lived beside a wealthy businessman. The merchant bought and sold rare oils for cooking, and from time to time would share them with his neighbor.

The dervish politely accepted these gifts, although he had no use for them. Not wishing to offend the merchant, the dervish would retreat to his humble home and pour the oil in a large clay jar hidden from view.

Using only a little oil now and then, the dervish seldom thought of all that he had collected. That is, he seldom thought about it until the day the jar could hold not a single drop more.

What shall I do with all this oil? he wondered. *My neighbor would think it rude that I have not used his gifts. To whom should I give it?* He wrinkled his brow with worry. *Perhaps I should find a needy family...but then again, I know of none—our village seems to be well off.* Fretting, the dervish tugged the tip of his beard. *And I can't give it to rich families ... that would disgrace them!*

---

[1] A dervish is a wandering Sufi, a religious person who lives simply.

He began to pace back and forth, back and forth across his small room, hands wringing behind him. *I can't just spill it on the ground; that is an insult to Allah and the blessings given to me.*

After some time, he stopped pacing. A smile crept across his face. *What about myself? I am the poorest person I know! If I sell this jar of oil—it must weigh at least ten pounds—and buy five sheep and graze those sheep in the hills this summer and each sheep has twin lambs ... well, in six months time I will have fifteen sheep ...* His eyes brightened as this idea grew. *And if I collect feed for next winter my sheep will become so fat that they will surely have one more lamb each and so in just one year's time I will have twenty good sheep ...*

Dizzy with these thoughts, he walked over to the window, leaned against his walking stick, and rested his gaze outside. But soon the dervish's large, imaginary flock returned. *And with the twenty sheep I can buy fine silk clothes, beautiful carpets and furniture... and with a little luck the size of my flock will double again in a single year...and I will furnish my house like a king and then a respected visitor will knock on my door and ask me to marry his beautiful daughter and ...*

Just then, the sound of children's laughter interrupted his fantasy. Stirring up a cloud of dust in the street, they kicked a ball between them. But the dervish only half-noticed the children before his thoughts continued in the same vein ...

My wife and I will have five healthy children and they will be scholars and be the happiest, brightest children in the world...and servants shall look after my flocks of sheep, and the children will go visit the sheep because it's very healthy for children in the countryside and fresh air is important for them ... a fight suddenly broke out in the street in front of the dervish. Howling in pain, one boy chased another in anger. A mother scolded them, but the dervish only half-heard ... *but what if the children misbehave sometimes—I suppose even mine could—and what if one tries to ride my most valuable sheep ... of course a servant would discipline such unruly behavior,* he muttered to himself, *but what if, what if the servant wasn't fond of my child and hit her for trying to ride that sheep ...*

The dervish suddenly found himself quite angry. "Why," he stammered aloud, "I'd fire that servant! I'd even go so far as to hit that servant for hitting my child!"

And the dervish, sputtering, red-faced with anger, raised his walking stick and smashed the clay jar as if that jar of oil was the servant.

The shattering crack woke the dervish from his daydream. Brought back to his senses, he surveyed his home. Oil oozed quickly, but harmlessly, across the mud floor: there were no cushions or carpets to be wrecked—yet.

Grateful that it wasn't blood on the floor, the dervish clasped his hands to his chest, bowed deeply, and whispered "*al hamdu lil Allah,* all praise to God!" With a wry smile and a cleansing shake of the head, the dervish renewed his pledge to keep his life simple for as long as he lived.

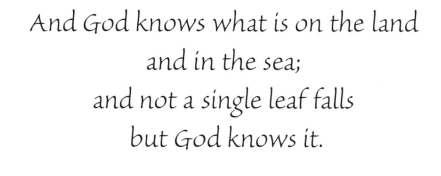

And God knows what is on the land
and in the sea;
and not a single leaf falls
but God knows it.

The Honorable Joha, Mulla Nasruddin
Hodja and the Pumpkin Tree

 The ever old but always young Mulla Nasruddin was involved in what he did best—relaxing under the shade of a walnut tree. Greeting friends as they walked by, enjoying his lunch of rice and lamb, he still found time to contemplate the wonders of Allah.

How generous is Allah, he thought, *to provide us with so many foods.* He smiled while picking up a walnut on the ground and examined it. *However, if I were God I would have done things better.* He looked over at the large garden of vegetables nearby. *Take the pumpkin for example. It is a huge fruit on a plant with no strength to hold it, while the tiny walnut comes from a tree with enough strength to hold a donkey. If I were God I would switch them and make pumpkins grow on trees.*

Just then he felt a tap on his head as a walnut fell from the tree. Looking at the object which had hit him, Mulla Nasruddin exclaimed, "Oh Allah, with what wisdom did You put walnuts on that tree. If it had been pumpkins, I would be sitting here with a huge lump on my head!"

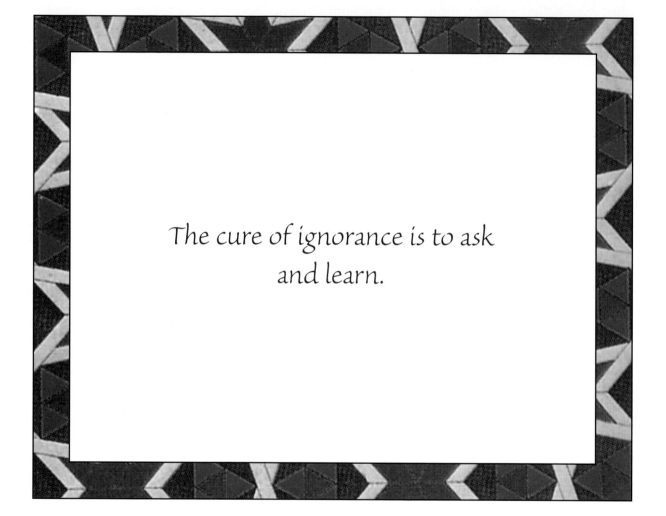

The cure of ignorance is to ask
and learn.

Words to Live by: A Tale from Iran

 Long, long ago, there lived a ruler of Nishabur who longed to be just, wise and generous; he was, however, the opposite. His temperament was as changeable as the wind: when things went the way he desired, he gloated and puffed about. When something unpleasant came to pass, he stomped and wailed in a childish fit. He played favorites in his court and held grudges for years. In short, he was a difficult, unhappy man.

But the ruler had one important virtue: he knew he needed to change. He recognized that his misery was his own doing. So one day he sat down to "make his hat the judge"—that is, he pledged to think seriously about his problem until it was solved.

After a little thought, it occurred to the ruler that his temper was likely the result of poor nerves, or perhaps, a weak heart. He summoned the best doctor in the land, hoping for medicine to cure his anger. The doctor felt his pulse, listened to his heart, examined his eyes, and tapped his knees to check the nerves.

At last, the doctor faced the Ruler of Nishabur and spoke solemnly: "I'm afraid there is nothing physically wrong with you." This was good news of course, but also bad news, for that meant the ruler's misery was not due to poor health.

The ruler bellowed, "You must have missed something! Of course there is something wrong with me!" He rose and stomped in a circle. "I think the problem might be that you are no good at medicine!"

The doctor waited for the ruler's temper to subside. Then he gently said, "No, the problem is nothing that an herb can cure. Doubtless, you have a problem, but I'm afraid it is a problem of character. Most likely, you were spoiled as a child and cried until you got your way. Hard as it may be, you must now grow up."

The ruler didn't much care for these words, but in fact, they stung with the truth. He listened. "What you must now do," continued the doctor, "is find the right spiritual medicine. Read every book of wisdom ever written. Listen to the advice of the greatest thinkers. Find a motto to live by that will give you patience and contentment so you do not become lost in joy or sorrow."

The Ruler of Nishabur took this advice to heart. "You're right," he finally admitted. "I should have done this long ago." So the next day he summoned to his court an imam—a Muslim cleric—and a scholar. He recounted his problem to them.

Said the imam, "What you must do is constantly remind yourself that life is brief; you must spend many hours in a graveyard, knowing that neither happiness nor *you* will last forever. Contentment and peace will come when you widen your perspective."

The ruler lost himself in thought briefly. "Those are good words, but I can't run to the graveyard every hour and continue to rule the country. I need something simple, something I can keep always with me."

Said the scholar: "The best solution then would be to surround yourself with learned men and women, and before making any decision, seek their advice. Issue orders only with their consent. This will prevent you from acting impulsively or unwisely. They will also help you to recognize your pride and they will offer solace for your sorrow."

The ruler gave these words some time to sink in. The imam and scholar waited. At last the ruler said, "No, that's not a good enough solution either. How can I be an effective ruler if I have to get the agreement of ten people before I open my mouth? No, this recommendation is also too complicated." And then he looked aside in shame. "I *do* understand the difference between good and bad," he said. "It's just that I get angry too easily or am so happy I make a fool of myself. No one trusts me." He looked directly at the two men. "I rejoice in others' misfortune if I can outsmart them. I get angry at the rain when it gets me wet. I pout when I'm not flattered. I'm mad when it's too hot and miserable if it's too cold." The ruler looked past the men, into the distance. "I always want something better than I have. No," said the ruler, shaking his head, "I must find a way to guide myself. I want something short and simple to inscribe on my ring which will never fail to guide me—a gem of wisdom that will work in every situation."

The scholar spoke up. "There's nothing wrong with your idea, Your Honor," he said. There are many who are wise and learned within the city. If you must have it quickly, I would suggest you hold an assembly right away."

"Yes," said the ruler. "This is the best idea yet. We shall send out letters and call it 'The Great Conference of Calming Words.'"

A week later the great conference began. Philosophers, poets, artists, scholars and imams crowded the room. One by one, each stood before the ruler, offering advice. Thick books were consulted, songs sung, poetry recited, sermons offered. It was a dizzying array. But the ruler was not yet satisfied, complaining, "No, that's too long," or "that phrase is too complicated," or "that motto is childish." Nothing seemed to suit the ruler and he began to lash out in frustration, just as he always had in the past.

Just then, a messenger arrived at the court. Although dressed in homespun clothes, there was something regal and wise about the way he carried himself. He stood to the side while the ruler read the message he had delivered. Meanwhile, the crowd began to grow unruly, pointing out the shortcomings of this or that advice. By the time the ruler had written a reply to the note, the messenger, a good listener, understood exactly why the assembly had been called.

As the ruler handed him the response, the messenger offered, "I believe I have a simple motto, sir, only four words long, which will meet your needs. With your permission, may I speak?"

At first the ruler hesitated. "Well," he finally said, "I don't see why not. Perhaps you know something these men don't." So the ruler hushed the assembly, requesting that they let the messenger address them with his four words of advice.

They protested. "This man can't even read. He wouldn't recognize the difference between the front of a book and the back!"

Another snickered, "He says he has a motto four words long which charts a course of wisdom in any situation? I don't believe it for a second. He's a fool!" A noisy chorus joined in agreement.

"Wait," said the messenger. "What you say is true—I am not learned. But have you found a motto for our ruler? If I offer one, then, what harm can it do?"

The ruler liked this kind of competition, and besides, he was beginning to feel rather desperate. "Go ahead," he said.

"Our ruler has asked," the messenger began, "for a short motto to guide his actions in every situation. It must protect him from pride when he is lucky and successful. Just as importantly, it must soften the blows of sorrow and disappointment." The messenger looked at the sea of stubborn faces in the crowd, then he faced the Ruler of Nishabur. "I know of four words which can achieve this," he paused and then spoke, "*this too shall pass.*"

Chaos broke out in the hall. "That is a foolish saying, and will make him spineless."

"How can that be a guide?" said another, "It doesn't show right from wrong."

"This is an old-fashioned way to look at things," shouted a third.

But throughout these disagreements, the Ruler of Nishabur was occupied in thought, gazing at the messenger. Eventually the ruler spoke, "Actually, in my view, these four words might be the best I've heard today. They will help me to reflect in every situation and they question a quick temper. They are soothing as well as simple. They will help me remember that all things are changeable. They remind me to accept the good with the bad, happiness with sorrow," he said.

The members of the conference were not pleased with the ruler's choice of the simple motto. Some reacted angrily, others sulked. At last the ruler announced, "Until better words can be found, these four words will be my motto."

He dismissed the assembly and sent the messenger away with the reward of a large pearl. Soon after, the Ruler of Nishabur had the words, *this too shall pass,* inscribed on a plain, gold band.

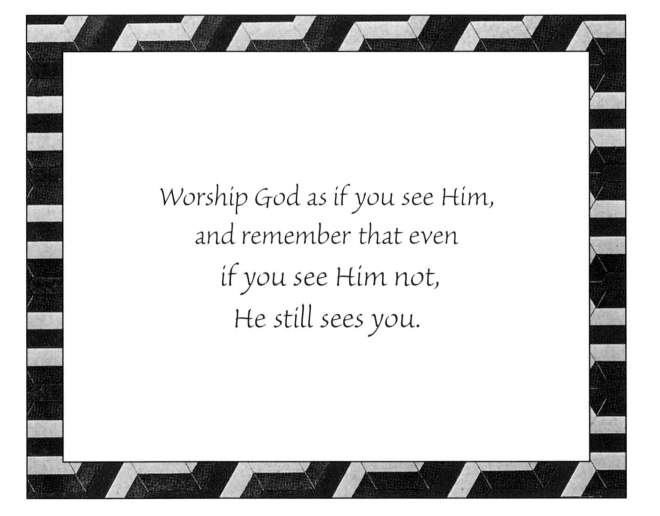

Worship God as if you see Him,
and remember that even
if you see Him not,
He still sees you.

Hajar and Ismael: From Hadith

 The Prophet Ibrahim (Abraham) was married to Sarah for many years but they seemed unable to have any children. Following Sarah's suggestion, he then married her servant Hajar. Ibrahim loved both of his wives, and was very happy when Hajar gave birth to a baby boy whom they named Ismael.

A few months later Ibrahim received a revelation from God, telling him to move Hajar and Ismael to a valley known as Mecca. The three rode by camel into the desert with a full skin of water and a leather sack of dates. Reaching the area that is now called Mecca, Ibrahim asked Hajar to sit under a small tree near the location of the first house of worship built by Adam, which had all but disappeared by this time. The area was now deserted, without even a source of water.

When he had settled Hajar and Ismael, Ibrahim started to ride off, on his way back home. Hajar followed him saying, "O Ibrahim! Where are you going, leaving us in this valley where there is no person for company, nor anything for us to eat or drink?" She asked him many times, but Ibrahim wouldn't look back at her. She then shouted, "Has God ordered you to do this?"

He turned, replying, "Yes, I am leaving you in Allah's care."

Content with this answer she said, "I am satisfied to be with Allah. He will not neglect us."

Ibrahim proceeded onwards, and upon reaching a place called Thaniya, he raised both hands, and prayed:

> O our Lord! I have made some of my offspring dwell in a valley
> without cultivation, by Your Sacred House (Ka'bah at Mecca) in
> order, O our Lord, that they may offer prayer perfectly. So fill
> some hearts among people with love towards them, and (O Allah)
> provide them with food, so that they may give thanks.

Hajar, alone with Ismael, nursed him and drank from the water that she had brought. But when the water was gone, both she and the child became thirsty. Ismael began to cry inconsolably. "I must see if I can find somebody to help us," she said aloud.

Hajar left her baby in what little shade there was, and headed toward the hill of Safa which was the nearest high point. She stood on it and looked, but there was no one in sight. She came down to the valley and ran until she reached the top of the next hill, Marwa. Not seeing anyone from there either, she began to run to and fro. Altogether she ran between the two hills seven times.

Then she thought, *I'd better go and check on how my baby is.* She found him on the brink of dying. Suddenly, she heard an unfamiliar voice, and she made herself to be quiet and listen. Hearing the voice a second time, Hajar said aloud, "O, whoever you may be! You have made me hear your voice; do you have something to help me?"

Suddenly Hajar saw the angel Gabriel digging the earth with his heel, until water flowed from that place. She made something like a basin of wet sand around it with her hands and was then able to fill the skin with water. Thankfully, after drinking the water she was able to nurse Ismael again.

Then the angel Gabriel reappeared and said, "Do not be afraid of being neglected, for here is the House of God which will be rebuilt by this boy and his father, and Allah never neglects His people."

Hajar and Ismael remained in the valley, and as time went on, many caravans stopped for the flowing water. Ibrahim came from time to time to make sure they were doing well. When Ismael was a grown man, the prophecy of the angel came true, and he and his father rebuilt the Ka'bah. Gradually, people came and settled until the site grew into the city of Mecca where the water of Zam Zam continues to flow to this day.

If you want to sleep in peace
beneath the ground,
make tranquil the hearts
of beings above it.

The Castle in Cordoba: a True Story
of King Hakim

Over a thousand years ago, King Hakim, rich beyond the dreams of many, ruled the country of Andalusia. One day, setting out on horseback, the king spied a forested hill overlooking the countryside just perfect for a new palace and garden.

The king sent his manservant to inquire about its owner, and discovered that an old woman lived there in a small cottage. He sent his servant back with a handsome offer for the land's purchase. The old woman refused: she wanted to live out her last days at home. The king doubled the offer, but she wanted no part of it.

Impatient to build his palace, the king commanded his soldiers to oust the old woman and set her up with a new home elsewhere. Soon, carpenters, stone masons and gardeners arrived

at the site and in a few years time, King Hakim had a new palace and a blossoming courtyard garden.

But the old woman had not forgotten the king's unjust possession of her property. She went to the Qadi, the chief justice of the land, with her complaint. The Qadi, knowing that justice often follows in the footsteps of patience, decided to wait for a solution to present itself.

Not long after, the king happened to invite the Qadi to the new palace. Gladly accepting the invitation, the Qadi piled a number of large, empty cloth sacks on a donkey's back, and arrived at the appointed time.

"What have we here?" asked the king when he saw the amusing spectacle of the Qadi leading a donkey into the garden courtyard.

"I would like to ask Your Majesty if I may take some sacks of earth with me from the renowned royal garden," replied the Qadi.

The king found no reason to deny the Qadi this unusual request. "Go ahead and be my guest," said King Hakim. "There's no shortage of dirt here!" and he watched the Qadi fill the sacks with rich soil.

Finally, the Qadi finished. He turned to King Hakim and asked for his help loading the full sacks upon the donkey. The king sprung to the task: he grasped two corners, the Qadi the other two. Together, they succeeded in raising the heavy sack only ankle high. Setting it down, readjusting their grip, they attempted again. And again. Try as they might, King and Qadi were unable to lift a single sack upon the donkey.

When the king looked entirely frustrated, the Qadi spoke up: "Sir, if you cannot lift even one sack of dirt now, on the Day of Judgment how will you transfer back the entire garden to the old woman from whom you unjustly took it?"

King Hakim blushed in shame. Realizing his great error, he sent for the old woman. When she was brought before him, he apologized: "I have wronged you terribly, mother. Please let me make amends. I beg you to take this palace and garden for your own."

The old woman stood silent for some moments. "Your Majesty," she said at last, "I do not want a palace. I would be grateful and happy if I could move back into my cottage and tend to my own garden again. *Inshaa Allah*, God willing, I still have some seasons left to appreciate it."

The King nodded in agreement. "*Inshaa Allah*," he said, "may you have many years left to enjoy it!" And indeed she did.

Good deeds are a shining light.

The Honorable Joha, Mulla Nasruddin Hodja, Affanti and the Donkey's Tail

 Once, long ago, a very wise man named Affanti lived in a province of China. Both kind and witty, he spent his days helping the poor and the unfortunate.

But the Emperor of China, both cruel and arrogant, became jealous when he heard about Affanti's popularity among the people. He had his soldiers arrest him and bring him to the palace.

Surrounded by guards, Affanti and his donkey stood before the emperor in his courtyard. "Affanti," the Emperor barked, "I've heard you are very clever. I will test you today." The emperor smiled wickedly. "If you can't answer my questions you will lose your life."

"*Inshaa Allah*, God willing, I will do my best to answer your questions," Affanti responded, with a humble bow.

"How many stars are there in the sky?" asked the Emperor.

Affanti pointed to the Emperor's chin and said, "There are as many stars as hairs in your beard."

"Then how many hairs do I have in my beard?" rejoined the Emperor.

Affanti grabbed the tail of his donkey, saying, "There are as many hairs in your beard as there are hairs in the tail of my donkey. If you don't believe it, count them for yourself."

Furious at the suggestion that his chin and the donkey's rump had something in common, the emperor shouted, "How dare you compare my beard to the donkey's tail!" He turned to the guards. "Take him and kill him!"

Affanti grinned. "I knew I was going to die. But now, not only do I know when I am going to die, I also know when you are going to die!"

This piece of news left the emperor stunned for a few moments. He called off the soldiers. "Tell me immediately, when am I going to die?"

Affanti answered, "You are going to die one day later than I. If you kill me today, you will die tomorrow, *inshaa Allah*, if God wills it."

The emperor paled with fear. "Affanti," he said. "I order you not to die! You must live for ten thousand years! I assure you that your every need will be fulfilled. You *will* live a long and healthy life." And the emperor heaped treasure upon treasure at Affanti's feet. A short time later, Affanti walked out of the palace with his head held high and his donkey loaded.

As soon as he was away from the palace, he gave all the treasure to the poor living alongside the road. After that, Affanti hopped on his donkey and continued his travels as he had begun: poor, humble, and content.

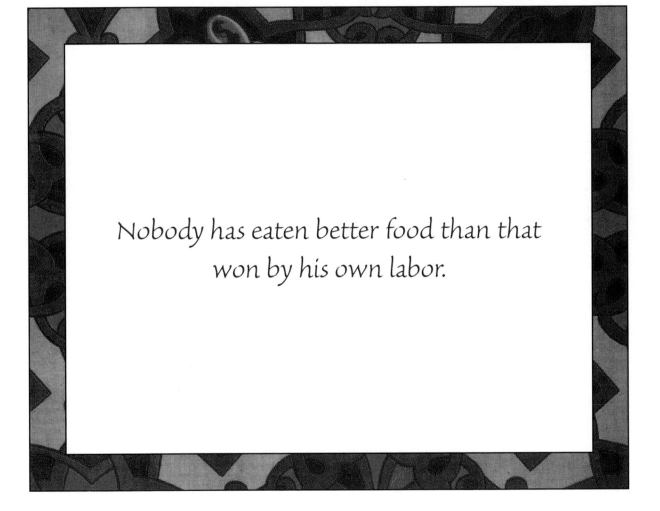

Nobody has eaten better food than that won by his own labor.

True Inheritance: A Tale from Iraq

 Kan ya ma kan: there was and there was not a kind, hard-working farmer, the father of several lazy, greedy sons. On his deathbed, the father told his sons that he had buried their inheritance, a treasure, in a certain field near the house. Soon after, the old man died.

Without delay, the sons hurried to the field. Although it was more labor than they were accustomed to, the sons dug the field up from one end to the other looking for the treasure. Alas, they found nothing. But it was early spring, and the land was alive with the first shoots and blossoms. Having already plowed the field in their search for treasure, the sons decided to plant wheat, and by mid-summer, they reaped an abundant harvest.

The lure of the gold, however, was never far from their minds. Thinking that they might have missed something from their first excavation, they unearthed the field from end to end a second time. Still, they found nothing. But it so happened that it was early spring again, and the land, in its myriad ways, hinted of coming fruitfulness. So the sons planted the field, and reaped another rich harvest by summer's end.

After several years of this same routine, the sons began to slowly change. They found that they could appreciate the changing of the seasons, the rhythms of planting and harvest and the satisfactions of their own labor. Gradually, the lure of the hidden inheritance grew distant in their hearts. They became honest, hard-working farmers, and soon came to realize that their father, in fact, had left them the greatest treasure of all.

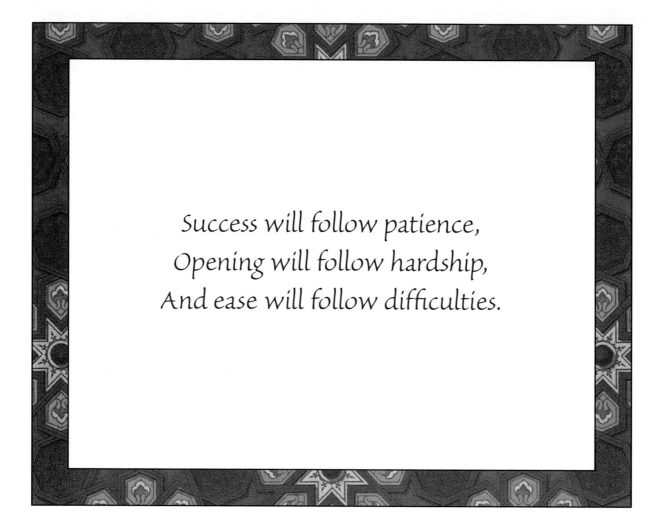

Success will follow patience,
Opening will follow hardship,
And ease will follow difficulties.

A Tent for the Emperor: A Tale from Turkey

 Once there was and twice there wasn't a girl named Fatimah, who lived in a city of western Turkey. Having lost her mother at birth, she was the lone and dutiful daughter of a spinner. Protective and kind towards his orphaned child, her father was also philosophical, and never missed an opportunity to talk with Fatimah about life. When business went well, her father seemed pleased enough, repeating what the Qur'an says: *the outcome of all things is ultimately up to God.* When money was scarce, the father seemed equally calm, smiled and said the same phrase, *the outcome of all things is ultimately up to God.* By and by, some of this patience rubbed off on Fatimah, and to others she seemed wise beyond her years.

One day, Fatimah's father invited her to come on a sea journey which he planned to take in order to find new customers. The father had in mind that perhaps, if their luck held, he would also find a young man of means—maybe even a prince—for Fatimah to marry.

Inshaa Allah, if God wills.

A few days after they set out to sea, a storm overtook the boat and capsized it. Fatimah woke to find herself cast upon a beach, the only survivor of the shipwreck. For better or worse, her injuries had caused her to muddle the facts of her life; she couldn't remember from where she had come, or who her aunts, uncles and cousins might be. Fatimah knew only four things for certain: her name was Fatimah; she was a spinner; she had lost her father; and the words of a particular phrase—*the outcome of all things is ultimately up to God.* Desolate and alone, hungry and thirsty, she wept. She vowed, however, to be patient in her faith, and hold on to the wisdom of those words as if they were water and bread.

A few days later, a kind and humble family found her stranded on the beach and offered to adopt her: she gladly accepted and silently thanked Allah.

Her new family were craftsmen who wove cloth. Fatimah, with years of experience using her hands for spinning, learned quickly. Day by day she improved her skill. Day by day she grew accustomed to her new family. Bit by bit, Fatimah grew happy again.

But we can never predict our fate. And so, once, while collecting shells on the beach, Fatimah's life changed yet again. A band of slave traders landed and carried her and some other captives off with them to Istanbul. Desolate, hungry, thirsty and orphaned a second time, she wept. But lodged in her heart she felt the presence of her father, repeating the words from the Qur'an over and over—*the outcome of all things is ultimately up to God.* She willed herself to be patient.

Several days later in Istanbul, there were only a few buyers at the slave market. Looking forlorn yet trustworthy, Fatimah was spotted by a businessman who had come for slaves to work in his wood yard. He purchased her to become his wife's maidservant.

Arriving back home, however, the businessman was informed that his largest cargo of masts had been pirated. No longer able to afford workers, he nevertheless resolved to keep the business going with just the three of them—his wife, himself and Fatimah.

Grateful for being rescued into a good situation, Fatimah proved once again adept at learning a new skill. Soon enough, the three of them had a thriving business of mast-making. Although she earned her freedom, Fatimah chose to stay on with the businessman and his wife, who appreciated her hard work and trustworthiness.

Not long after, the man requested she oversee a delivery of masts to a place off the coast of China. Fatimah, despite her fear of the sea, agreed to go. *After all*, she thought, *what are the odds of my being shipwrecked twice in a lifetime?* And then there were the words she carried with her like precious jewels—*the outcome of all things is ultimately up to God.*

However, it came to pass that once again Fatimah caught the brunt of a brutal storm, the boat sank and she found herself washed ashore in a foreign land. "How can this be?" she cried. "Why does one person have luck and another not?" But she felt the strength of her father's words in her heart. Picking herself up, Fatimah headed towards the nearest village.

Now it so happened that China, where she landed, had a legend of a woman that would land on its shores and sew a magnificent tent for the emperor. Back then, no one in China knew how to construct such a tent, but travelers had seen large and elaborate tents, and the emperor wanted one of his very own.

To ensure that the fabled woman would not be missed, every year, each emperor, as far back as anyone could recall, had sent a herald to every village, town and city. And so it was at this time, when the emperor's crier had the ear of the village, that Fatimah appeared on the beach. In a short time she was brought to the court of the Emperor of China.

"Lady," the emperor asked through an interpreter, "Can you sew me a tent?"

Her head bowed in deference, Fatimah replied, "I think so, your Majesty." She had never before made a tent, but Fatimah, with her years of faith and patience, knew that she could figure it out.

Fatimah first asked for rope, but none could be found of the right sort. Drawing upon her old knowledge of spinning, she collected flax fibers, and spun the needed rope. Next, she requested some sturdy cloth for the body of the tent, but alas, none could be found that was just right. Drawing upon her skills as a weaver, she wove a durable, stout canvas. Finally, she needed large, straight tent poles. Once again, none were exactly right for her purposes. So, using her skill as a mast-maker, Fatimah cut and whittled and fit poles of perfect proportion.

At last, with all the proper materials at hand, Fatimah quickly constructed an elaborate, magnificent tent. When the emperor saw it, a smile spread across his face; at last, the legend had come true! In return, he offered Fatimah any treasure in his vast kingdom. Fatimah chose simply: "I would just like to settle here, your highness," she said, "in China, the place where Allah has delivered me."

Fatimah's fame soon spread from one end of China to the other. Offered the hand of a prince, she accepted. Eventually Fatimah was surrounded by her children, and her children's children, each of whom could recount her great adventures and the words: *the outcome of all things is up to God.*

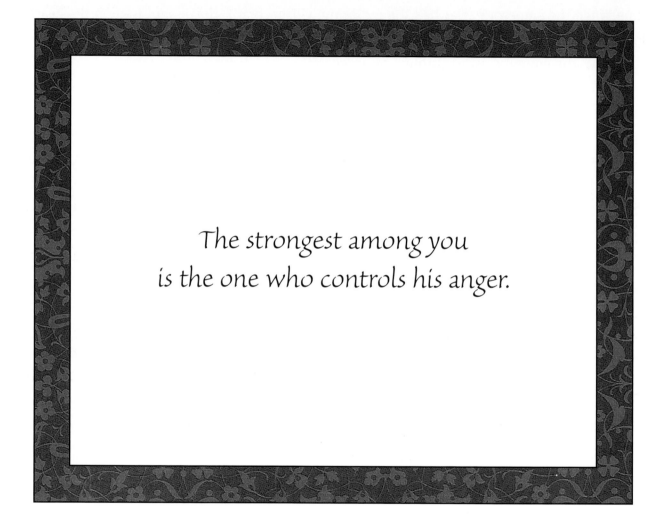

The strongest among you
is the one who controls his anger.

The Parrot and the Grocer: A Tale from Iran

 One day or another, a grocer spied a beautiful parrot in the village market and purchased it for his store. His business had been lagging of late. He gambled on the bird's spectacular colors and gift of speech to bring in more customers. The grocer hung the bird's cage in the doorway, and things came to pass just as he had hoped: people couldn't help but stop to admire the bird and delight in its prattle. Business improved and the grocer, elated, named his bird "Sweet Tongue."

Now Sweet Tongue was, in truth, no ordinary parrot. He didn't just mimic people, he actually seemed to listen, understand and converse. In fact, after some time the grocer considered the parrot a good friend and treated him accordingly, allowing the parrot to fly freely about the shop. Soon, Sweet Tongue and his friend, the grocer, had the most successful business in the city, and the grocer decided to expand the store.

He borrowed a large sum of money and the shop was built, boasting pyramids of bottles and mountains of goods. And as before, Sweet Tongue had the freedom to fly around the shop and converse with the customers. Business couldn't have been better.

One morning, however, as the grocer put his key into the shop door, a strange odor wafted to his nose. Opening the door, he discovered a disaster: nearly every bottle in the shop had been toppled and shattered. Rice and lentils mixed with expensive oils and spices littered the floor. Atop all the mess Sweet Tongue perched, preening his feathers.

Without a moment's thought, the grocer grabbed the parrot and beat him so hard about the head that the bird nearly died. "Look what you've done by your flying about!" he shouted. "You've ruined me!" Locking the parrot back in its cage, the grocer sat down on the floor and wept, unsure of how he'd ever recoup his losses.

The days passed and the store got cleaned, but one thing refused to return to normal: Sweet Tongue. Having lost all his head feathers from the beating, he cowered in the back of his cage and refused to talk. The grocer tried everything he could imagine: he tempted Sweet Tongue with delicious nuts and sweet meats; he apologized; he hired a musician to try to lift the bird's spirits; he removed the cage door. Nothing worked. The bird simply would not be cajoled out of its despair.

Finally the grocer resigned himself to this new state of affairs, and did his best to make the business as successful as before. But customers that previously came to see Sweet Tongue, purchasing a little something out of courtesy, stopped their visits. Others too, were less drawn to the store which now exuded a gloomy mood. Business flagged. The parrot continued his long silence until the day a dervish with a very shiny, very bald head walked through the door.

A raspy voice suddenly cut through the musty air. "Hey baldie!" shrieked Sweet Tongue, "How'd you end up with no hair? I bet you broke a store full of bottles too!"

The dervish looked around until he found the source of the voice. He grinned, spying the bald parrot.

"So," said the dervish, "because I too am bald, you assume we've got the same story, eh?"

At this time, the grocer, hearing Sweet Tongue speak again, ran over to the two and eagerly watched. "Of course," said the parrot. "What else could it be? You must have made someone very, very angry by the look of you. Not a single hair left on your head!"

The dervish chuckled and Sweet Tongue prattled on. The dervish had some wise words to say to the parrot about the problem of making assumptions too quickly, but the grocer wanted only to hold his bird. *"Al hamdu lil Allah!* Thanks be to God! My friend, the parrot, speaks again!" he cried aloud, picking the bird up, gently stroking Sweet Tongue's feathers and showering him with kisses.

A few minutes later, the grocer noticed that the man had gone. He put the parrot down, ran out to the street and tried to find him, but the dervish had disappeared. No one in the marketplace recalled seeing a bald dervish that day. But it was said that the grocer, a wiser man ever after, never—not even once—lost his temper again. And Sweet Tongue, having at least a year's worth of chatter to catch up on, never—not even once—stopped talking to his friend, the grocer.

True servants of God
are those who walk humbly
on the earth and say: "Peace!"
to the ignorant who accost them.

The Head and the Lute: A True Story of Bayazid Bustami

 Late one evening under a full moon, Bayazid Bustami, a religious teacher, walked by a drunkard sprawled along the roadside. As Bayazid neared, the drunkard became quite feisty, bellowing the most hateful and filthy curses at him.

Bayazid did not respond, but curiously, his silence seemed to stir the drunkard further. Rising, he pulled out his lute, and angrily smashed it on Bayazid's head. The lute shattered into a hundred pieces, yet Bayazid did not fight back. He simply continued walking home, dabbing his bloody wound from time to time.

The next morning Bayazid sent his servant—with money and a heaping tray of deserts—back down that same road to find the drunkard. He also instructed his servant to deliver the following message: "Last night my head was responsible for breaking your lute. I apologize. Please purchase a new one with these *dirhams*. I also found your tongue to be quite unpleasant and bitter. Please eat all of these deserts to sweeten it!"

Ashamed of his behavior, the drunkard dusted himself off, came straightaway to Bayazid to beg his forgiveness, and gave up drinking for good.

What is wisdom?
Do what you should do
when you should do it.
Refuse to do what you should not do;
and, when it is not clear,
wait until you are sure.

The Clever Kantchil: A Tale from Indonesia

 It began a long time ago, this war between the crocodiles and the mouse deer. It began with a crocodile named Buwaya, who lived by the banks of a river.

It so happened that one day, as Buwaya prowled along the shore in search of food, a large tree fell upon his back and pinned him to that very spot. Thrashing and making quite a racket, he was heard by Karbau, the water buffalo, who soon came down to investigate.

As soon as Buwaya saw the buffalo he pleaded, "Ai, ai! Take this tree off of my back! I cannot wriggle free, and I will surely die without your help!"

Karbau was kind, and did not hesitate. He took his long horns and pushed the tree, inch by inch, off of the crocodile's back. Yet when Buwaya was free, he still didn't move. "Help me again," said the crocodile. "I am so weak and hurt that I cannot get myself back into the water." Again, Karbau didn't hesitate, but gently used his powerful horns to nudge the crocodile into the water.

"Thank you," said Buwaya, "but the water's still too shallow. My back hurts too much to swim. Can you help me get a little deeper?" Karbau obliged. "Deeper still?" begged the crocodile, and soon Karbau found himself chest high in the river.

At this point, you can probably guess what the crafty crocodile had in mind—a water buffalo dinner. Buwaya snapped himself into action and grabbed hold of the Karbau's leg with his claws and teeth.

"Ai!" screamed Karbau, "What do you think you're doing?"

"I'm hungry," mumbled the crocodile, without opening his mouth.

"But I've just saved your life!" said Karbau. "What kind of selfish creature are you, that you would take the life of your rescuer?"

"A hungry, smart animal," retorted Buwaya. Now Karbau was neither weak nor little. He began to make quite a racket attempting to spear the crocodile with his great horns. Amidst the grunts and groans and snapping, Kantchil, the little mouse deer, ran to the river bank to assess the commotion.

"What is going on here?" he demanded.

Karbau fiercely backed himself towards the shore. "I saved this miserable creature's life! I took a tree off of his back and now he shows his thanks by trying to eat me!"

"Not so!" said the crocodile. I was already eating, a tree fell on me, and so I took a break. I'm just back to where I started."

Kantchil stepped closer to the two animals. "I think this matter requires a legal judgment."

"Well, who will decide?" asked Buwaya.

"I will be the judge," said Kantchil. "Now, please cease your activities. Let's re-enact the situation, so I can determine who is right and who is wrong."

Letting go of the water buffalo's leg, the crocodile slid onto the bank, near the fallen tree. "Well now," said Kantchil, "show me what happened, and in the order it happened."

Karbau said: "I heard a great noise and a cry for help, so I came down to the shore and found the crocodile stuck under this tree."

"I'm not sure I quite understand," said Kantchil. "Would you please show me exactly how you found Buwaya?"

"Exactly like this!" and with that Karbau raised the tree slightly and put it square upon the crocodile's tail again.

"Ai!" yelled Buwaya. "Take it off of me!"

Kantchil asked the water buffalo, "Is this exactly the way you found him?"

"Yes," replied Karbau.

"Is this the way Karbau found you?" Kantchil asked the crocodile, who was struggling in discomfort.

"Yes!" he shrieked. "Now please get this off of me."

"Ahh, well then," said Kantchil, "It is quite obvious that you did indeed attack your rescuer. I rule that the water buffalo should go free, and you, Buwaya, will stay just where you are."

Now, as it's been told over many generations, this tale of Buwaya, Karbau and Kantchil was just the beginning. The crocodiles declared war on the clever mouse deer and have been at it ever since.

Another time, a day came when Kantchil smelled something tantalizing in the breeze from the other side of the river. Having eaten much of the fruit on his side of the river, Kantchil knew that the breeze sang of irresistible mangos and bananas, heavy and ripe. He stepped into the reeds by the side of the river to get an even stronger whiff.

"War on Kantchil," shouted a nearby crocodile, lunging for the deer.

The crocodile's teeth landed on an underwater root, not on the mouse deer's leg, but Kantchil screamed, "Ai, ai! Let go of my leg! You will drown me!" The crocodile's jaws clamped tighter on the root and the mouse deer scampered away.

Kantchil trotted farther downstream until he came to another crossing place. Right off the shore, looking like a bridge, floated a large, long, black object. "Are you a log or are you a crocodile?" shouted Kantchil. But the object, a crocodile, was old and crafty: he remained silent.

Kantchil had an uneasy feeling. "I say," said Kantchil, "if you're a crocodile, you would float downstream like all crocodiles do. If you're a log, you will float upstream, as all logs do." So at this point, the long, black crocodile began to swim slowly upstream.

"Hah!" said Kantchil. "Everyone knows that logs cannot swim upstream! Farewell, you imposter!" And Kantchil retreated to a high spot on the shore. Soon, however, that same smell of ripe fruit wafted by and encouraged him to think of a new plan.

In a booming voice, Kantchil shouted, so that all in the vicinity could hear: "Allah has declared that today is the day the number of crocodiles in this river must be counted and written down. Today is the day of Allah's census!" Slowly, one by one, crocodiles floated to the surface of the water until the river teemed with them, packed side to side, end to end.

"Now," bellowed Kantchil, "Do not move even so much as a tail until the census is taken. We must not confuse God's numbers!" Kantchil jumped on the first crocodile's head, "One, in the name of Allah!"

He leaped onto the next crocodile, "Two, in the name of Allah!" Counting as he jumped, he shouted, "Three, four, five and six, in the name of Allah!"

"In the name of Allah," chorused the crocodiles.

"Seven, eight and nine, in the name of Allah!"

"In the name of Allah," sang the crocodiles in their gravelly voices.

"Ten, eleven and twelve, in the name of Allah," shouted Kantchil.

"In the name of Allah," repeated the crocodiles.

By the time Kantchil had reached one hundred, he had only a short step to land. And there he was, back on dry ground, on the far shore. "I declare that Allah's census is now officially over!" he shouted at the crocodiles. With a bounding leap, Kantchil then turned towards the fruit that had beckoned him, only to find that it lay overripe and spoiled on the ground beneath the trees. "*Aiee*," he thought, "*Allah is not pleased with this trick*," and resolved to avoid misusing God's name when dealing with the crocodiles in the future.

Although these are only two tales of the war between the crocodiles and the mouse deer, it is certain that the scuffles will continue, and we will hear new stories as they float their way down the river.

Knowledge is better than wealth.
Knowledge guards you,
while you have to guard wealth.
Wealth decreases by spending,
while knowledge multiplies by spending.

The Best Investment: A True Story of Rabia ar Ray

The grey haired man at the door was weary from his travels but thankful to be home. A captive for many years, he had only recently been freed. As he knocked, he wondered if his wife and son were still living there. Would they recognize and welcome him?

The young man who opened the door was polite but not inclined to let the stranger enter. "Who are you?" asked the old man.

"I am Rabia ar Ray," the younger man answered politely, "And who, might I ask, are you?"

Hearing voices, his mother came to the door in time to hear this last question. With tearful eyes she gasped, "He is your father, Farukh. Let him come in!"

The next morning, Farukh, sleeping in his own bed for the first time in years, woke early to perform the required cleansing before morning prayers. "We should wake Rabia," he said to his wife, "so he can walk to the mosque—the *masjid*—with me."

"Rabia is already at the *masjid*," she replied. "He always goes before the time of the morning prayer.

Farukh left the house and headed towards the mosque, amazed, and pleased, to see hundreds of people also headed to prayer before dawn. *Mashaa Allah—wonderful are the ways of God! So many people attending the masjid early in the morning!* The mosque, in fact, was so crowded that Farukh was forced to stand up against the back wall. He could hear an inspiring talk, but couldn't see who the speaker might be.

After the prayers, as everyone left the *masjid*, Farukh looked, but still could not see his son. He went back home alone. Rabia entered a while later while his father was discussing the family's finances with his mother.

"I left you with quite a sum of money. I hope that you've had enough money for your needs," he said to her.

"The money has taken good care of our home and the two of us," she replied. I have invested all of the rest," she smiled and reached for Rabia's hand.

"I see evidence of everything but the investment," Farukh said, looking around the room. "These are the same furnishings as when I left. What has been the return?" he asked. "How much has the money increased?"

Mother looked at son. "I'm certain the increase is 100,000 fold. I hired the best scholars to tutor our son." She smiled at Rabia. "100,000 is the number of people who have come to the mosque these many months to hear him talk. A wise scholar now, he is the one that you heard speaking in the *masjid* today."

His eyes bright, Farukh replied, "*Al hamdu lil Allah*, all thanks to God, this is the best investment anyone could make."

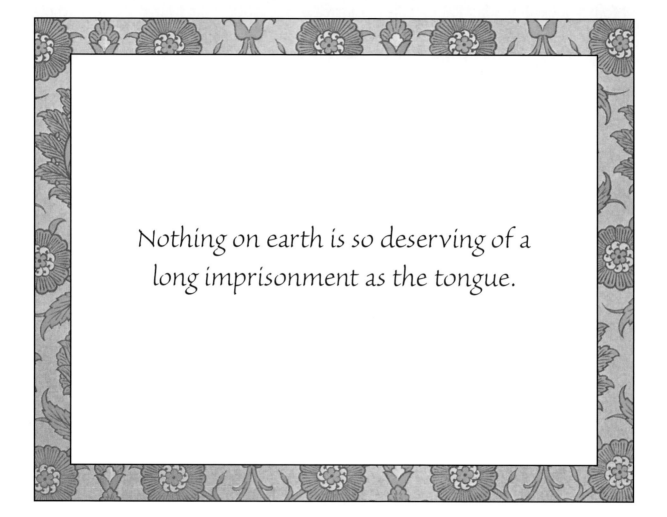

Nothing on earth is so deserving of a
long imprisonment as the tongue.

The Price of a Secret: A Tale from Azerbaijan

The storytellers say that Alexander-the-Great, King of Macedonia, had a terrible secret: his great, big ears. His ears were so large and so odd that he wore a hat day and night. He entrusted only a single person, his barber, with the secret, certain that he would be laughed from his kingdom if others knew. But finally, the day came when Alexander-the-Great had a second problem: his old barber had fallen sick and was close to dying.

"Who can possibly replace you?" asked Alexander. "I must have someone as trustworthy as you, someone who will never, ever, disclose the royal secret."

The old barber replied, "I think there is a young man, Vahid, in your service who is honest and loyal and will not give away the secret. Vahid is who I recommend."

Alexander-the-Great held out as long as possible, but alas, the old barber died, and so Vahid was employed. Standing behind the king, Vahid readied his tools to cut the king's hair, but when he removed Alexander-the-Great's hat, the scissors clattered to the floor. Vahid stood astonished behind the king.

"If you ever dare tell anyone this secret—anyone—I will have your tongue ripped out, your eyeballs plucked, and finally, your head cut off." He paused for effect. "Do I make myself clear?" said Alexander-the-Great.

Vahid, mustering all his courage, coughed out a weak, "Yes, Your Majesty. I understand." He picked up his tools and proceeded to cut the king's hair very, very carefully.

Vahid had promised to keep the king's secret, but alas, felt so terrified he could neither eat nor sleep. Visions of his own head, without eyes or tongue, rolling down the street haunted him. Frightened that he might slip the secret to others inadvertently, he stopped talking altogether. Soon enough, Vahid, sleepless and exhausted, sickened. To get better, he knew he must rid himself of the secret. What could he do? Who could he tell? It's hard enough to keep one's own secrets, but to hold on to those of others is an even greater burden.

Finally, Vahid had an idea. He would travel far outside the city and shout it to the sky or a tree or a bird—he had to get it off his chest. So the very next day, he made his way to the sheep-herding meadows outside the city and came upon a well. He looked. No one was around. Vahid bent down into the well, looked into its cool darkness, and shouted, "Alexander-the-Great has huge, big, ugly ears!" *There!* He thought. *I am done. I've said it and no one knows it!* Vahid walked back home, happy for the first time in many days.

A few weeks later, a shepherd stopped to rest by that same well. Watching his flock nearby, the shepherd drank some water from the well and then plucked a blade of grass sprouting near its rim. Holding it between his fingers, he made a sort of reed whistle and blew into it. To his great surprise, it wasn't a reedy tune that came from the grass, but instead the words: "Alexander-the-Great has huge, big, ugly ears." The shepherd blew again, and again, with the same results. He smiled, amazed.

Now it so happened that at the same time the shepherd entertained himself with the whistling grass, Alexander-the-Great, hunting in the countryside, heard the royal secret from across the meadow. Immediately, he had the shepherd arrested. Sure that he must be a friend of Vahid's, he also had the young barber brought before him. The shepherd told how he had simply made a whistle from a blade of grass sticking up from the well.

"Absurd and impossible!" shouted Alexander. Then he turned to Vahid. "Confess that you have told the royal secret to your friend here!" he commanded.

But Vahid denied ever having met the shepherd before, and described to Alexander exactly what he had done and where he'd done it.

"You shouted the secret into a well?" Alexander asked.

"I swear," said Vahid, "that's all I did. No one was around to hear."

"But why?" asked Alexander.

"I could no longer keep the burden of your secret to myself, and I knew if I told it to someone else, they too would need to share the burden. So, I chose to tell the well."

Alexander remained thoughtful for some moments. He then ordered that another blade of grass be brought from the well and that the shepherd fashion another reed whistle. It was done. The shepherd blew into it, and out piped "Alexander-the-Great has huge, big, ugly ears," just the same as the first whistle had.

The king turned to Vahid and said, "You may still be my barber if you wish. Now you no longer have this secret to keep." Vahid bowed slightly and thanked the king.

"And you," said Alexander to the shepherd, "are also free to go." The shepherd gave the king the whistle and happily returned to his sheep in the countryside.

Then Alexander-the-Great had the best calligrapher in the land pen the following words in gold ink, which the king hung over his bed for the rest of his years:

REMEMBER ALWAYS THAT YOU
ARE YOUR OWN BEST CONFIDANT;
FOR EVEN A WELL,
WHICH SEEMS LIKE A SAFE PLACE,
MAY BETRAY YOU.

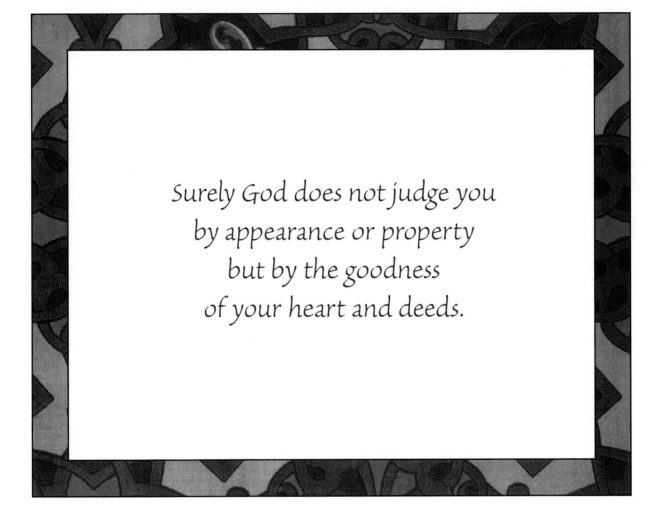

Surely God does not judge you
by appearance or property
but by the goodness
of your heart and deeds.

The Honorable Joha, Mulla Nasruddin Hodja Feeds His Coat

 Long, long ago, during the fasting month of Ramadan, Nasruddin Hodja was invited to his wealthy neighbor's house for a dinner party. Late coming back from his field on the day of the party, he debated what to do. *If I go home and change I will be late for the dinner. Is it better to be late, or a little dusty? And besides, I haven't eaten all day.* He decided to go in his farming clothes.

Nasruddin Hodja brushed himself off and knocked on his neighbor's door. Entering, he saw that everyone else had dressed up in their finest. Trying to make conversation with the other guests, he began to wonder if he had suddenly turned invisible: no one would talk with him. When he spoke pleasantly to a man standing beside him, the man looked up and down at his clothes, and sidled away to another guest. After a second, and then a third similar incident, Nasruddin Hodja quietly left the party and hurried home.

He changed into his finest coat and his largest turban. Knocking again at his neighbor's house, Nasruddin re-entered the party. But this time, everyone had something to say to him. He found himself the center of the party; even the host asked Nasruddin Hodja to sit beside him.

As the first plate of kofta—meatballs—was passed to him, Nasruddin stuffed a few in his pocket. Next came a platter of chicken: he grabbed a leg and dropped it into his wide sleeves. Snatching a few of the stuffed grape leaves, he tucked them in his turban. Soon, the eating and conversation stopped as all the guests stared at Nasruddin Hodja.

"What on earth are you doing?" asked his host.

"It is quite obvious to me," replied Nasruddin Hodja, "that since everyone ignored me until I put on this fancy coat, it is my clothes who have been invited, not me. Therefore I am feeding my coat."

Give now of your gold and wealth,
for soon it will pass from your grasp.
Open the door of your treasure today,
for tomorrow the key
will not be in your hands.

Know Yourself: A Tale from the Middle East

 Kan ya ma kan: there was and there was not a man known far and wide for his generosity. One day, sitting with his friends sipping coffee in the village square, a poor woman approached him with a small request for money to feed her child.

"Of course!" he replied, and without hesitation plucked coin after coin out of his pocket, piling them into the woman's hand until they spilled on the ground.

Overwhelmed with this show of kindness, the woman began to weep. She bowed her head in gratitude. "May Allah bless you, Sir. You have saved my child's life." She carefully placed the coins in a small cloth sack. Glancing up a last time, she thanked him with a frail half-smile.

When she was out of earshot, the man's friends probed him with questions: "Why did you give her so much money?" asked one.

"That was foolish. Don't you think she will tell all her friends?" asked another.

"A line of beggars will be at your door tomorrow morning!" warned a third.

"Just yesterday, you gave your *zakaat*, your charity," said a fourth. "You weren't obliged to give her any. Why did you do it?"

The generous man kept silent until their indignation ran its course. At last they quieted down.

"While such a poor woman may be pleased with just a little money from me," said the generous man, "*I* couldn't have been." He looked from friend to friend. "Unless I give her what I am able to, *I* won't be happy. She may not know me, but I know myself."

And the group of men, thoughtful and contrite, said no more about it.

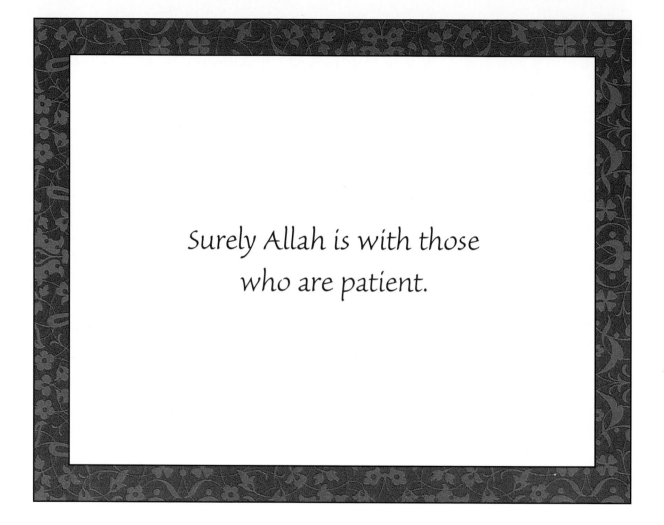

Surely Allah is with those
who are patient.

Infant Jesus: From the Qur'an

 The Prophet Imran and his wife were blessed to have a child during their old age. In recognition of this miracle and out of thankfulness, they dedicated the child to the service of God while still in her mother's womb. The child was born a girl, whom they named Mariam (Mary).

As a girl dedicated to the service of God, she grew up studying and worshiping in the temple, away from the distractions of daily life.

One day, the angel Gabriel appeared to her and said: "I am a messenger from Allah. I am here to announce that you will have a son."

She answered him, "How can I have a son, when no man has ever touched me and I am not an immoral woman?"

The angel replied, "So it shall be. Your God says, 'It is easy for Me, and We will make him a sign for mankind and a show of grace to them.' And this matter has already been decreed." With his message delivered, the angel disappeared.

As Mariam's pregnancy developed, she left the temple for a distant oasis so the people wouldn't see her pregnant and gossip about her. When it was time to deliver the baby, the labor pains were very strong and she eventually found herself at the base of a palm tree. As the pain became almost unbearable, she cried out, "I wish that I had died before this and was unknown and forgotten."

Then a voice called from under her, "Do not grieve: Allah has provided a cool stream beneath your feet, and if you shake the palm tree, ripe dates will fall for you. So eat and drink and cool your eyes. And if you see anyone ... you shall not speak."

She named the baby Isa (Jesus). After she recovered from the birth, she returned to the town from which she had come. When the people saw her, carrying her son in her arms, they said, "Oh Mariam, you are coming with something unbelievable to us...Your father wasn't a wicked man, and your mother wasn't an immoral woman." Mariam was still not speaking, so she pointed to the baby. The people were incredulous and said, "How can we talk to a baby?"

To their surprise, Jesus answered them, saying, "I am indeed a servant of Allah ... He has commanded me to pray and give alms as long as I shall live. He has commanded me to honor my mother...Peace was upon me the day I was born, and the day I shall die and the day I shall be raised up again."

Such was Isa, the son of Mariam.

Do they not observe the birds above them
spreading their wings and folding them?
None could hold them except
the Compassionate Allah;
surely it is He Who watches
over all things.

What the Birds Know: a Tale from Iran

Many, many years ago, in southern Iran, there lived a holy man, a dervish. The people of his city had named him "Danadil" or "wise-heart," because of his extraordinary wisdom and good nature.

Like every devout Muslim, the time eventually came for Danadil to make *hajj,* his once-in-a-lifetime pilgrimage to Mecca. Packing all that he owned in a small rucksack, along with a few coins for supplies, a little food and water, Danadil set out. Although it would take him weeks to walk the caravan route to Mecca, Danadil, cheery with the thought of reaching his life's goal, trod through the sandy wilderness alone and unafraid.

On the third day, it happened that by sunset he had not reached a village in which to spend the night. Far from any town, he came upon an old campsite, now a den of thieves.

When they spied the lone traveler, the thieves rejoiced. Here was easy prey! The dervish had no protection and a rucksack full of goods. Without hesitation they surrounded poor Danadil.

The dervish saw that he was trapped; nevertheless, he boldly asked, "What kind of men are you that attack a poor, old man traveling alone?"

"We are bandits, of course!" replied the bearish leader, bowing his introduction. "We are happy to make your acquaintance." The group of thieves laughed. "Since we are already disgraced before God, what does it matter if we attack a young rich man or a poor old one? We must do what we can to stay alive!"

Danadil implored them, "If you must take the few things I have, then do so. But let me make my holy journey to Mecca. Let me continue on with nothing but the clothes I wear."

The group of men guffawed. "Ha! Should we believe that you will not tell the authorities about us? Before long we would be out of business." Towering over the dervish, a tall, thin man stepped forward and grabbed Danadil by the collar. "No, your journey is to end today, where no one will see what has become of you."

Danadil held his gaze. "You may have the power to kill an innocent, but misfortune will forever be on your heels. You can't hide from justice; I may die, but justice never does."

The gang sniggered. "If you think justice can find us in this wilderness," replied the tall man, "you are greatly mistaken. Prepare to die old man!"

Danadil looked at the circle of faces. Clearly, no one would be coming to his aid. But the sky above caught his attention, suddenly tinged with sunset's rose and orange. And just then, a cloud of starlings flew overhead. "Take pity on me birds!" Danadil called to them. "Be my witness! I am a victim of Godless men without mercy. Only you and God know this terrible deed! May you bring justice upon each man."

"Fool!" said a man, "You hope to be saved by birds! What is your name old fool?"

"Danadil."

At that, the men shook with laughter. "Oh, well, the name of 'wise heart' shall be forever changed to 'old fool.'" And with those words, the thieves killed him. They divvied up Danadil's belongings and by the next morning had moved on, leaving his unburied body by the side of the road.

A few days later, Danadil's corpse was discovered by some travelers from his home. Distraught over the death of their beloved dervish, they buried him and built a small memorial of stones.

"Surely the death of an innocent man shall be punished," they comforted themselves. They brought the sad news back home and the townsfolk murmured about it for many days.

But one day followed upon the next. Eventually people ceased mourning and went about the business of their lives, the upsetting death of Danadil rarely spoken of anymore.

Spring arrived. Along the river, blossoming trees filled the air with perfume; carpets of wildflowers lined the riverbank and birds moved from tree to tree overhead. Soon the townsfolk went picnicking in the nearby countryside.

It so happened that on one particular day, the thieves that had killed Danadil also lounged by the river, not far from the picnickers, in the shade of a large tree. Above the thieves, hundreds of birds chattered in the branches. Whether it was just because the tree was the largest—or because of some other reason—the racket of bird song and the bird droppings falling upon them began to catch the thieves' attention.

"Oh ho!" joked one. "This must be the work of old Danadil. Oh the terrible justice of bird droppings!" They chuckled.

"Yes, what a punishment indeed," said another.

But the townsfolk had heard Danadil's name mentioned, and began to listen carefully to the thieves' banter. Soon, their suspicions were confirmed that the thieves had some special knowledge of poor Danadil's disappearance. A few slipped away to fetch the authorities while the murderers joked and snoozed.

The authorities arrived, surrounding the thieves. And as it goes amongst their type, their stories began to contradict each other and unravel. Arguments and lies quickly snared the men in their own net, for it was obvious they had had a hand in Danadil's death.

So whether it was more than coincidence that the starlings crowded on that particular tree on that warm spring day, or more than luck that the townsfolk overheard the talk of the thieves, will never be known. All that we know is that God's justice prevailed and the murderers, each and every one, were indeed punished.

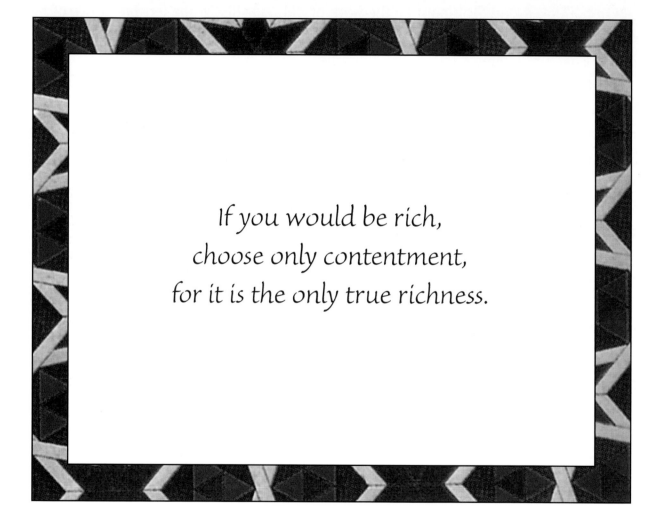

If you would be rich,
choose only contentment,
for it is the only true richness.

The Water Pot and the Thief: A True Story of Rabiah Al Adawiya of Basra

 Famous for her saintly life, Rabiah of Basra owned nothing but a sleeping mat, a brick on which to rest her head, a Qur'an and a water pot. One night, a robber, unaware of whose house it was, slipped into Rabiah's home. Looking around, he soon discovered … nothing—nothing at all to take.

Just as the thief was turning to leave, Rabiah spoke up, "If you are indeed a robber, surely you cannot leave empty-handed."

Startled, the thief replied, "But there is nothing to steal!"

Rabiah stood up and handed him her water pot. "Take this water and ready yourself for prayer. Perform your *wudu*, your ablution, as the Prophet Muhammad ﷺ has taught us."

The thief, looking confused, tentatively accepted the water pot. Rabiah pointed, "Go into the side room there and pray. If you do this regularly, you will never be empty-handed or poor."

The robber did as he was told. When Rabiah heard him begin his prayers, she raised her gaze to heaven and entreated the Lord, "Allah, a thief has entered my humble home and found nothing. Now that I have shown him the way to your mansion, do not keep him from it; do not bar him from your goodness and bounty." She lay back down, the sound of his prayer soothing her back to sleep.

The thief, having performed just two rounds of prayer, found to his surprise that it brought him immense joy. And so he continued.

At sunrise, many hours later, Rabiah rose and walked into the side room. There she found the thief seated, reading from the Qur'an.

"And how was your night, my friend?" asked Rabiah.

"It went quite wonderfully," he answered. "I saw myself standing before God, and He accepted my repentance and forgave me."

Rabiah smiled, "I believe you are now—and forever—a very rich man," she said.

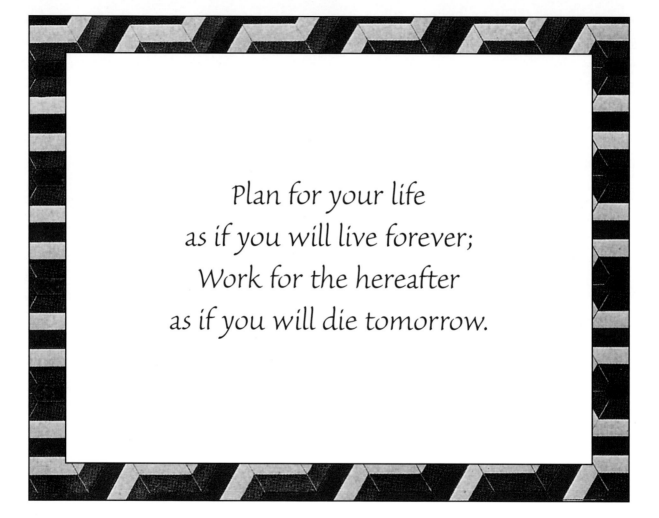

Plan for your life
as if you will live forever;
Work for the hereafter
as if you will die tomorrow.

The Storm: A Tale from Iran

Once, long ago, there was and there was not a dervish, a wise man, who boarded a boat to make a journey by sea. Recognized by his dervish's turban, he soon found himself with a long line of passengers before him, each hoping for a bit of advice. But despite the variety of concerns, the dervish said the same words to each person: "Try to be aware of death, until you know what death is." No matter the problem brought to him, his answer remained, "Try to be aware of death, until you know what death is." By the time the boat departed, the line had vanished because truthfully, few people like that sort of advice.

Several hours after leaving port, a fierce storm overtook the boat. Great curls of water crashed over the deck, and the sails were shredded by the gusting wind, until it seemed the ship had little chance. Throughout the storm, passengers clung to each other, wailing in terror, or pleading with God to save them.

Meanwhile, in the bow of the ship, mostly unnoticed, stood the dervish. Gripping the gunwales on either side, he looked about him with curiosity and great attentiveness.

When the storm at last subsided and patches of blue sky returned, the passengers, one by one, slowly realized that the dervish had remained calm and tranquil during the ordeal. They soon crowded around him.

"Didn't you know how close we were to death? Weren't you afraid?" asked a fellow, wide-eyed from fright.

A woman, soaked and shivering, asked the dervish, "Didn't you realize the danger?"

"Yes, of course. I have always known this about the sea," said the dervish. "On the water, there is never more than a plank that divides us from death." He looked kindly at the woman. "But has it ever occurred to you that on land, day or night, storm or not, there is even *less* than a plank between you and death?" The dervish smiled serenely, confident that the people would finally understand.

Truth brings peace to the heart.

Trustworthy Traveler: True Story of Abdul Qadir Jilani

 Born in 1077 CE near the Caspian Sea, Abdul Qadir had a deep desire to increase his knowledge. He scoured his city of Jilan, sitting with every scholar he could find. But alas, the city was small, the scholars were few, and the wealth of knowledge lay in the wonderful city of Baghdad far to the south. To complicate matters, his father had died, leaving him and his mother in poverty. His duty to his mother bound him to her, but his deep desire to seek knowledge pulled him away.

Oh, what a mother he had! She loved her only child so, and prayed to Allah that he would be guided rightly. But what *was* the right path? Should she keep Abdul Qadir with her, or help him in his search for knowledge? Although the classes of the Baghdad scholars were free to rich and poor alike, the travel there was both dangerous and costly. If he went, it would mean buying a donkey or camel to ride on, and joining a caravan for safety through the harsh desert, where robbers were known to frequent the route.

They decided he would go, eighteen year old Abdul Qadir, to the House of Wisdom, *Beit al Hikmah,* in Baghdad. It took time and sacrifice to save for it, but at last his mother paid the initial costs of the journey. She then took the remaining money, forty dinars, and sewed them into the lining of Abdul Qadir's home-spun coat to avoid detection. Then she prayed that Allah would protect her son and guide him. She bid him farewell with the warning to remember the value of truth, to be truthful in all things, great and small.

As it happened, after some days of travel, robbers indeed attacked the caravan. Only the two guards of the caravan were armed and the robbers quickly overcame them. They searched and questioned each of the merchants for anything of value, but ignored the poor young man in the ragged coat. Finally, as they prepared to leave, the thieves probed the group with one last question, "Do any of you have anything else of value with you?"

Abdul Qadir spoke up: "Yes, I have."

"Oh, really?" they scoffed, "And what great wealth do you possess?"

"I have forty silver dinars with me," Abdul Qadir replied.

"And where is this money of yours?" the robber chief asked, laughing with the other men at this ridiculous young man.

"It is here, in the lining of my clothes," answered Abdul Qadir, patting his coat.

Feeling the coat's lining stuffed with coins, the robber chief looked puzzled. "I don't understand. Why would you tell us about the money? If you had said nothing, we wouldn't have found it!"

"I promised my mother never to lie about anything. Even if you hadn't discovered my lie, God would still know," answered Abdul Qadir.

Shamed, the robber chief and his men fell silent at the simple honesty of this young man. Filled with remorse, the robber chief ordered his men to return all the stolen goods to the travelers, and permitted the caravan to go on its way.

Abdul Qadir continued on to Baghdad. In time he became a learned scholar known as Imam Abdul Qadir, whose writings and teachings we still learn from today. And the robber chief and his men? Well, they turned their lives around and became a force for good.

And among His signs is this:
that Allah created for you mates
from among yourselves,
so that you may dwell with them
in tranquility; and he has put love
and mercy between you.

The First Supporter: A True Story of Khadija bint Khuwailid from Hadith

 Khadija was a wealthy businesswoman who needed to hire someone she could depend on to do her trading and to care for her goods when her caravan reached Syria. After a brief search, she hired Muhammad ibn Abdullah ﷺ, known throughout Mecca as 'The Trustworthy.' He accepted the position and performed his tasks responsibly.

After he returned with an excellent recommendation from those who had accompanied him, Khadija decided he would make the best of husbands—even though he was fifteen years younger. She asked Muhammad to marry her. He agreed. Together, they had six children and their business continued to flourish.

One day, Muhammad and Khadija's lives changed forever. Muhammad had gone to a cave on a nearby mountain to meditate, something he did frequently. This time, however, the angel

Gabriel appeared, filling the cave, and then the horizon, with his enormous presence. He said he had a message from Allah for Muhammad: this message began the revelation of the Qur'an.

When the Angel disappeared, Muhammad raced home. He was trembling as he said to Khadija, "Cover me!" She covered him with a blanket until he became calm.

"O, Khadija! What is wrong with me?" he said. "I am afraid that something bad has happened to me." He then described his overwhelming experience in the cave.

As she listened to his words, Khadija did not share his fears. She realized that something tremendous and awe-inspiring had happened to her husband, but was sure it was something good. She comforted him by saying, "No, it's not possible that it's something bad. It must be good news! By Allah, He will never disgrace you, for you are good to your family and relatives, you speak the truth, help the poor and the destitute. You serve your guests generously and help those in distress."

Khadija felt sure that Muhammad had received a true message from God. Seeking to reassure him, she asked him to go with her to see her cousin, Waraqa who was knowledgeable about Jewish and Christian scripture.

Khadija said to Waraqa, "Listen to the story of Muhammad, O, my cousin!"

Waraqa asked, "What have you seen?" Muhammad described what had happened to him. Waraqa then said, "This is the same angel Gabriel whom Allah sent to Moses. I wish I were young and could live up to the time when your people will turn you out."

Muhammad asked, "Will they drive me out?"

Waraqa replied, "Every prophet of God who said something similar to what you have said was treated with hostility. If I live until you have this problem, then I will support you strongly."

Waraqa died soon after he met with Muhammad. However, Khadija was convinced of Muhammad's prophethood and never wavered in her support of her husband. When the Prophet Muhammad was commanded by Allah to call the people to worship one God alone, Khadija did not hesitate to express in public what she had known in secret for some time. "I bear witness that there is no god except Allah," she said, "and I bear witness that Muhammad is the messenger of Allah."

With that one public statement, Khadija lost her position as one of the most prestigious people in Mecca and became an outcast. Even so, she refused to hide, and made a point of going with her husband to the Ka'bah in the center of town for prayer. Her clear thinking plus her generous giving of time and wealth were an enormous help to the small group who declared their faith in public. Some of her money went to free slaves who had embraced Islam and were being cruelly treated because of it.

Eventually all the members of Muhammad's tribe who had kept him from harm, and all the poor Muslims, were driven out of Mecca and forced to live in a small ravine in the nearby mountains. Here, the Muslims were exposed to bitterly cold winter nights, and later the fiery hot days of summer with very little food and shelter. No one was allowed to buy or sell with the Muslims. Due to being from a different tribe and wealthy, Khadija was not forced to join them. However, it was unthinkable to her that she not be with, and support, her husband and the other Muslims. Knowing that it would be especially difficult for her due to her advanced age, she nevertheless moved out to the ravine.

After three very long and difficult years, the boycott was lifted and the Muslims were allowed to re-enter the city, but the years of hardship had taken their toll. Khadija's intellect and faith remained strong, but her body could not recover from its deprivation, and she died soon after.

Some years later the Prophet Muhammad said of her, "She believed in me when no one else did; she accepted Islam when people rejected me; and she helped and comforted me when there was no one else to lend me a helping hand."

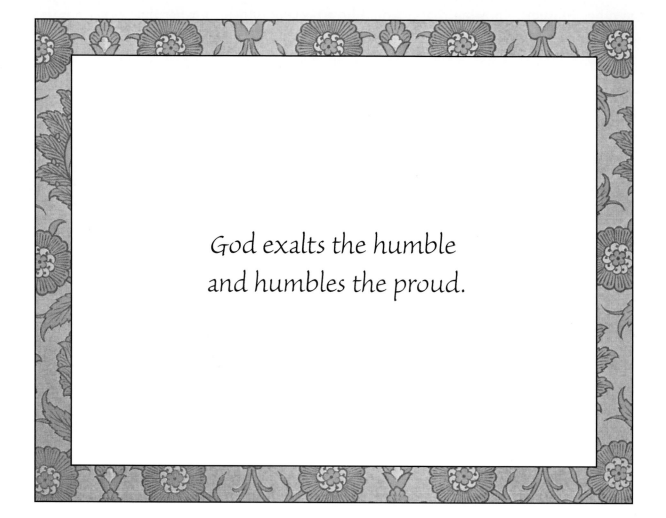

God exalts the humble
and humbles the proud.

It Is So: a Tale from Mali

 Long, long ago, a man named Seidu lived in the village of Gob. Like the other men of his village, he hunted to provide meat for his family. Unlike the other men, Seidu took credit for everyone's success. Seidu's wife, Ladi, would often ask, "Were you the best hunter today?"

Seidu, standing just a bit taller, would always reply, "It is so. The others were able to catch meat only because of me. *I* chased the lion; *I* threw my spear at the jaguar; and *I* caused the elephant to run away. Because of my courage, the others had luck."

On one occasion, a scout said that enemies were approaching the village. Seidu went along with a group of men to stop the enemy, but he was careful to stay in the back for safety. When they returned, Seidu brushed the dirt off his hands, hung his spear on the wall, and waited for his wife to ask about the battle.

"Did you turn the enemy away?" asked Ladi.

Seidu puffed up his chest: "When the enemy approached, I ran out in front, straight toward one hundred armed men. My courage frightened our enemies so much that they will never again come close to our homes." Ladi's eyes grew wide. Seidu continued, "Everyone knows now that Brave Seidu is the most courageous of all warriors. What do you say about this, wife?"

Ladi answered, "It is so."

Soon after, it happened that a woman died in a nearby village and the women of Gob wanted to attend the funeral. They needed protection for their long journey. Ladi spoke up, "Brave Seidu, my husband, is the fiercest of all the warriors. He will accompany us through the forest."

Ladi approached Seidu, "Since you are the strongest and most fearless of warriors, the women think you should be the one to take them through the forest. What do you say about this, husband?" Seeing no way to avoid this assignment without being called a coward, Seidu smiled and nodded, as if to say, *it is so*, and then swaggered into the hut to prepare his weapons.

The next day, Seidu and the women of Gob set out. Not long into the journey, they were spotted by their enemies. The foremost among the men pointed, "Look at that man strut like a rooster! He thinks he can protect all his hens!" The men sniggered.

Another spoke: "Let's give him something to deal with and see just how brave and calm the rooster remains." Silently, the men scattered into the bushes and trees by the side of the trail.

The women of Gob laughed and chatted among themselves as they neared the ambush. At a whistling signal from the men, they were encircled. Seidu, seeing he was vastly outnumbered, did nothing but shout, "Run for the trees!" to all the women as he also started running. But enemies had hidden among the trees, so Seidu and the women of Gob found themselves unable to escape. One and all were taken prisoner.

The leader spoke up, and addressed Seidu's wife. "What is your name?"

"Ladi" she replied.

He answered, "Ladi is a beautiful name that the women of our tribe also use. Because your name is Ladi, no harm will come to you." He stepped in front of the next woman: "What is your name?" Seeing that the name Ladi brought special protection, she replied, "My name is also Ladi." The enemy leader said, "As I said already, Ladi is an honorable name. We will not hurt you either." As he continued to ask woman after woman, he received the same answer.

At last he turned to Seidu: "It is very unusual for the women in a tribe to all have the same name. In our village, each woman has her own special name." He shook his head, befuddled. Then he faced Seidu. "So, Mr. Rooster, is your name the same as that of all the hens?"

Seidu paused and stared at the ground, hiding his panic. "Yes, I, too, am called Ladi. That is also my name," said Seidu, looking up briefly, and then at the ground in disgrace. The men burst out laughing.

"That cannot be your name!" said the leader. "Ladi is a woman's name. You hold a spear as a man would. Are all the men in your village also called Ladi?" the leader asked, a twinkle in his eye.

Seidu replied, "No, only the women are named Ladi."

"And so," said the leader, "How is it that you are also Ladi?"

Seidu squirmed, no longer able to meet the gaze of villager or enemy. "Well, appearances are like a mask: you can't always trust them. I, too, am a woman named Ladi."

This was too much for the gang of men. Rolling on the ground, they laughed until breathless. After a time, the real Ladi spoke up: "He is not Ladi, he is Brave Seidu, the most courageous of warriors. He is not speaking the truth. He is the famous Seidu."

The crowd quieted. Seidu spoke, "Yes, it is so," he said, attempting to stand a little straighter.

One of the men said, "It is said that Seidu claims he is the bravest of all."

"No," said Seidu. "This is no longer the case. Seidu *used* to be the most courageous of all men. But now, Seidu is just the bravest man in his village." The men guffawed, and thus began a new round of laughter at Seidu.

Eventually, the men had laughed so hard, and felt so satisfied that the rooster had been put in his place, that they no longer cared to take any captives. With a wave of his hand, the leader sent the villagers back home. "Good bye Ladi! Good bye!" the men joked, as they watched Seidu and the women from Gob file off.

Back in his village, Seidu found he could no longer step outside his hut without ridicule: "Oh hoo! Ladi come out, Ladi come out!" the villagers chided him.

After many days of this, Seidu asked his wife to deliver a message to one and all: "Formerly," she said, "Seidu was the most fearless man in the village, but now he has decided this is no longer the case. Seidu now agrees only to be as brave as other people."

And from then on, the people of Gob stopped teasing Seidu, and he lived contentedly, careful not to brag or boast. When fortune smiled on him, and he brought meat home to his family, Ladi would say, "*Al hamdu lil Allah,* thanks be to God that our stomachs will be full!"

And Seidu would reply, "Yes, we are most grateful. It is so."

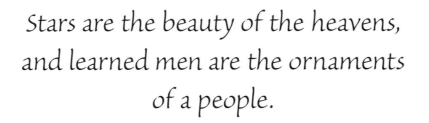

*Stars are the beauty of the heavens,
and learned men are the ornaments
of a people.*

Gate of Knowledge: a True Story of Ali ibn Abu Talib

 Six year old Ali was happy to go live with his older cousin, Muhammad ﷺ and his wife, Khadija. Long before Ali had been born, Muhammad was or-phaned and had lived with Ali's family. Now that Ali's father was struggling to feed his children, Muhammad had asked Ali to join him.

There were many reasons Ali liked living with his cousin, and not just because there was plenty of food. Curious about everything, he was also learning to read and write—something very unusual for a boy at that time.

For a number of years Ali simply enjoyed living in the household of his cousin, but then something happened that made him begin to take a more serious look at life. His cousin, Mu-hammad, became a prophet. Ten-year-old Ali felt that he needed to choose: to declare himself a Muslim or not. At first he said he wanted to discuss it with his father, Abu Talib, but then decided that he was intelligent enough to make his own decision. Ali was the first child and the second person to accept Islam.

His father asked him, "What is this religion you are practicing?"

"O father," replied Ali, "I believe in God, and in Muhammad as the Messenger of God, and I have accepted all that he has received from heaven. I pray to God with him and follow his religion."

Abu Talib then told his son, "Since he leads you only to what is right, follow him and keep close to him."

From then on, Ali spent as much time with the Prophet Muhammad as possible. Ultimately, he was known as the most learned person in the community, described by Muhammad as the Gate of Knowledge.

He was often one of the people who wrote down the revelations that his cousin had just received. Later he became an official scribe of the Muslim community. He wrote down the treaties the Muslims made with other tribes and groups, and wrote, on behalf of the Prophet Muhammad, the letters sent to the emperors of Byzantium and Persia and other heads of state.

Ali married Fatimah, youngest of the Prophet's daughters, and was beside Muhammad for the rest of the Prophet's life. As the Muslim community grew in Madinah and surrounding areas, the people increasingly brought their disputes for the Prophet's just decisions and many times he would ask Ali to settle the cases.

Some years after the Prophet's death, Ali, now Imam Ali ibn Abu Talib, was chosen as the Caliph—leader of the Muslims. Continuing to live in the same simple lifestyle, he was as dedicated to governing as he was to learning.

Among his words of wisdom, Ali ibn Abu Talib, may Allah be content with him, said: "A man who lacks knowledge should not shy away from asking about what he does not know, and a man of learning should never be too shy to admit his ignorance by saying, 'Allah knows best.'"

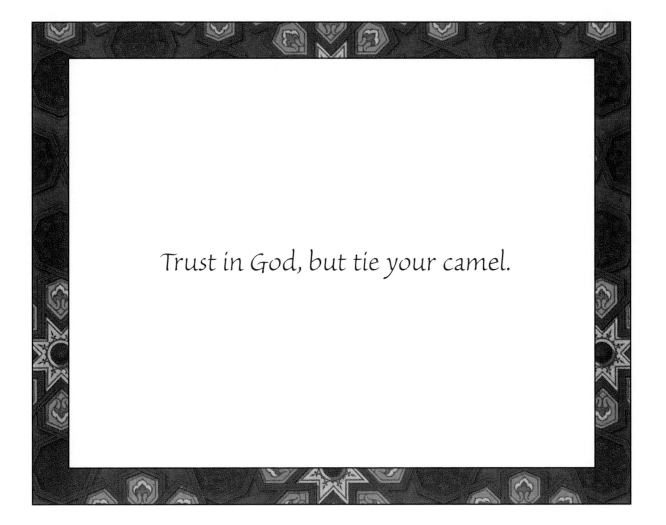

Trust in God, but tie your camel.

The Best Witness: From the Hadith

 The Prophet Muhammad ﷺ told this story: Once a man of the tribe of Israelites asked another of his tribe to lend him 1000 gold dinars.

"I agree to lend you the money, but I require witnesses as is usual," the lender said to the merchant.

"God is sufficient for a witness," answered the merchant.

"I accept that," agreed the lender. "But I will need a surety, someone who will guarantee to pay back the loan, in case you do not return from your travels."

"God is sufficient as a surety," the merchant responded.

"That is truly spoken," agreed the lender. "I will lend you the thousand dinars, to be paid back within the time we agree upon."

The merchant traveled across the sea to a distant land. After completing his business, he looked for passage on a boat that would enable him to return quickly and pay off the loan by its due date. Alas, there was no boat sailing in that direction for some time.

"With God as my witness, I must repay my debt," worried the merchant. "How can I get the money back on time?" Looking around he noticed a piece of wood that had been washed ashore. This gave him an idea, and he proceeded to hollow out a hole in the wood. He inserted the 1000 dinars and a letter to the lender, and then sealed the hole tightly.

He took the wood to the seashore and prayed, "O Allah! You know well that I took a loan of one thousand dinars from the lender. He asked for a witness, and I told him that God was sufficient as a witness, and he accepted You. He then demanded a surety from me, but I told him that Allah's guarantee was sufficient and he accepted Your guarantee. Truly I have tried to find a ship home so that I could pay his money back on time. However I cannot find any, so I hand over this money to You." He then threw the piece of wood into the sea and watched until it drifted out of sight.

The due date arrived and the lender went down to the sea to find whether a ship had arrived bringing his money. He saw no ship, but his eye fell upon a piece of wood that would be useful as firewood. Upon arriving home he proceeded to saw the wood into usable pieces. Imagine his surprise when a hole was revealed, full of a large sum of money and a letter addressed to himself!

Meanwhile, the merchant had continued his search for a way home and finally found a ship. As soon as he set foot in his town, he hurried to the lender's home. "As God is my witness," he hurriedly explained, "I swear that I tried every way to find a ship so that I could return your money on time. The one I just arrived on was the first I could find, and here is the 1000 dinars that you loaned to me."

The lender pushed the money away and asked him, "Have you sent something to me?"

"I just told you I couldn't find any boat before this one which I came on," the merchant replied.

The lender responded with a smile: "On your behalf, Allah has delivered the money you sent in the piece of wood. So you may keep this other money and depart on the path of righteousness."

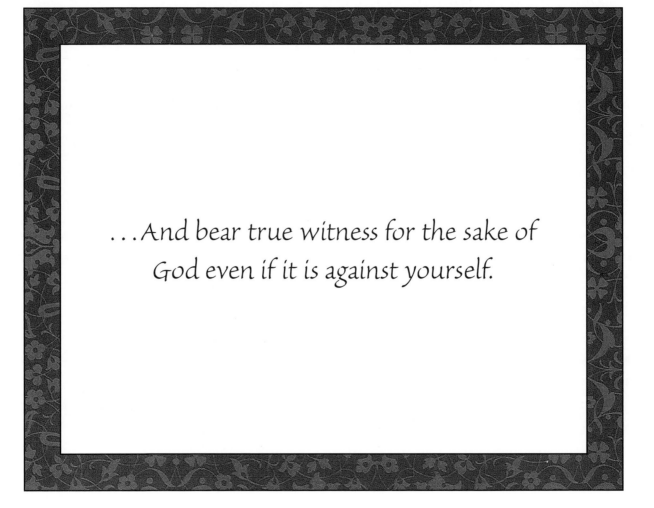

. . .And bear true witness for the sake of
God even if it is against yourself.

The Honorable Joha, Mulla Nasruddin Hodja and the Judge

 Once there was and twice there wasn't a small town whose judge was often drunk. One night, stumbling into a ditch by the roadside on his way home, the judge lacked the presence of mind to go any farther. He flung off his fine turban and silk coat, curled up, and called it a night.

Nasruddin Hodja and his student, Ahmed, out walking that same night, on that same road, happened upon the sleeping, snoring judge, oblivious to all. Nasruddin gathered up the judge's clothes and continued on his way.

The next day, Nasruddin Hodja was seen in town wearing the judge's costly cloak and turban. Without delay, Nasruddin was brought before the judge to answer charges of theft.

"Do you claim that these fine clothes belong to you?" barked the judge.

"No sir," replied Nasruddin most politely.

"Well, then, why are you wearing them? Why don't you return them to their proper owner?"

"I would gladly return them if I could only find the owner," said Nasruddiin. "You see sir, last night, my student and I came upon a dreadful scene, offensive to all good Muslims." The judge began to squirm. Nasruddin continued: "A man was so drunk he had taken off his clothes and fallen asleep half-naked by the side of the road. I thought I should protect his possessions from thieves by safekeeping them. I will gladly return the clothing as soon as the man, *inshaa Allah*—with God's help—can be found."

Clearing his throat, the judge found no easy reply. "Well ... er ... we ... er ... I mean to say, just what kind of man would disgrace himself so?" he stammered. "We shall hear no more of this silly problem. Be gone!" And the judge dismissed the case.

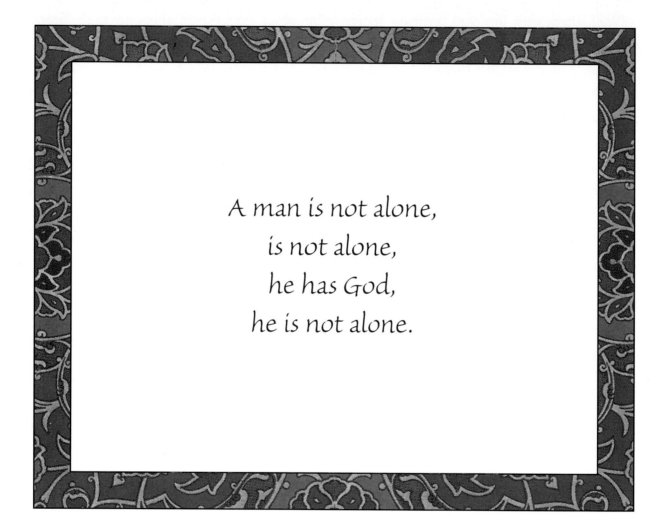

A man is not alone,
is not alone,
he has God,
he is not alone.

The Web and the Dove: from Hadith

 Forced to flee from assassins in Mecca, the Prophet Muhammad ﷺ and his companion, Abu Bakr, went southward to hide. Going away from, instead of toward their known goal, Madinah, they threw their assassins temporarily off the chase.

Under cover of night, the two men slipped away from the city, heading directly to the Cave of Thawr. After many hours walking, they climbed a steep hillside and scrambled into the cave. A cool quiet enveloped them.

For three long days the pair remained hidden while their assassins looked and looked, searching in Mecca and to the north. During this time, the Prophet Muhammad spent his time in prayer; Abu Bakr attended to their safety. Each night, Abu Bakr's son brought them news of their pursuers; by day, a servant grazed sheep in the nearby hills and delivered food, concealing any tracks to the cave with the flock of sheep.

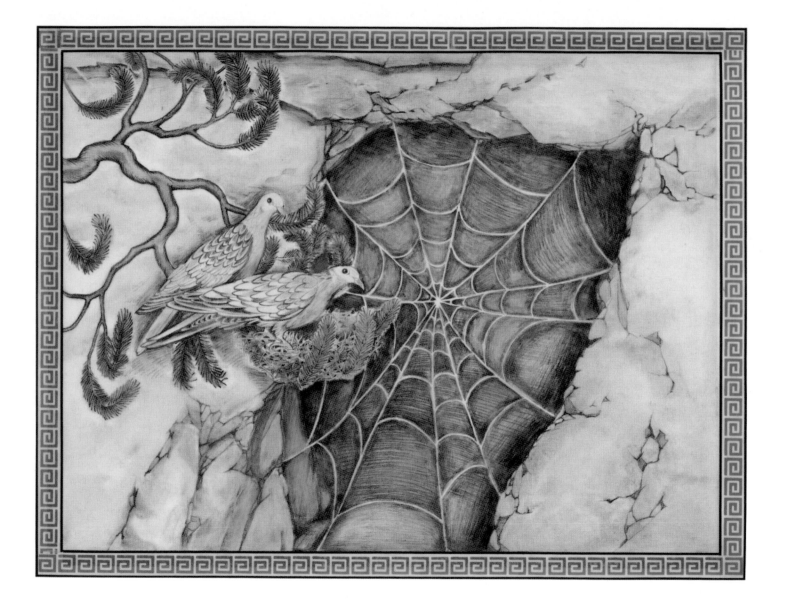

142

Exasperated with their fruitless efforts to the north, the young men chosen to kill the Prophet finally headed southward. They knew of the cave and guessed that the two men had sought refuge there. Armed and ready to kill, they approached a shepherd in the vicinity of the cave and asked if he had seen the Prophet Muhammad and his companion.

"Perhaps they are within the cave," answered the shepherd, "but I have not seen them."

Their voices reached the cave entrance from the valley floor. Abu Bakr withdrew to the back of the cave and whispered aloud his fear to the Prophet.

But the Prophet responded, "Do you think we are alone? There is a third with us," by which he meant God is ever-present.

When the first of the assassins reached the mouth of the cave, he stopped. There, spanning the entrance, a delicate spider web quavered in the sunlight, and a large bough, nesting a pair of wild pigeons, blocked the cave entrance.

"Why haven't you gone inside?" The group of men shouted from below.

"They could not be hiding in there," said the leader. "Had they entered," he explained to the others, "there would be no nest and the spider's web would be torn."

Convinced that the cave was empty, the men turned away, climbed back down the hill and continued their search elsewhere.

Not everything that is great in size
is great in value.

True Worth: A Tale from Syria

 Kan ya ma kan: there was and there was not a powerful sultan who yearned to make his kingdom the most honest in the world. Consulting with his chief judge, the *wazir*, the sultan hatched what he thought to be the perfect plan.

The very next day, the sultan's crier was sent from one end of the kingdom to the other—from the crowded city market to the farthest pasture—announcing a new, strict policy of absolute honesty. "Anyone caught telling a lie will face the stiffest fines from the Sultan," hailed the crier. "This policy is effective today, immediately."

The next part of the Sultan's plan called for a little spying. Disguising themselves as travelers, the sultan and his *wazir* planned their first visit. They chose the richest merchant in the city.

As is the custom in the Muslim world, the travelers were warmly welcomed into the merchant's home. The men settled onto cushions, and out came trays laden with dates and figs and sweet steaming tea.

Graciously serving his guests, the merchant awaited any questions that they might have.

"Excuse me sir," the sultan began, "but you look quite youthful for being so very successful. Exactly how old are you?"

The merchant hesitated, but then replied, "I've had twenty wonderful years, *al hamdu lil Allah*, thanks be to Allah."

Seeing that the merchant was well past twenty years, the sultan glanced briefly at his *wazir*, thinking that he had already snagged the first liar.

The *wazir* then asked, "And how many children do you have sir?"

"I have a single, praiseworthy son," answered the merchant.

Having heard of the merchant's many sons, the sultan felt more and more sure of the merchant's dishonesty. He boldly probed, "And how much wealth have you accumulated in your years?"

The merchant, still the polite host, politely answered: "For Allah's sake I have seventy thousand *dinars*." Now this was a great deal of money, yet not the full amount the merchant was reputed to have. In silence, the disguised men winked at each other, anticipating that the rich merchant would make the perfect example of dishonesty for the rest of the kingdom. But they had to be very sure; they had to check the records after the visit.

So the sultan and *wazir* continued their charade for the time being. The three men discussed the state of the surrounding lands and notable things of the times. Several pots of tea later, the conversation wound to an end. The sultan and his *wazir* stood and thanked the merchant for his generous hospitality and hastened back to the palace to check the facts. Sure enough, the records proved a very different account than the merchant's own words. The *wazir* dispatched two soldiers to bring the merchant to face charges for breaking the new law.

Surrounded by a council and his *wazir*, the sultan sat proudly at the head of his palace court, anticipating the success of the new edict. The merchant was brought before them, appearing somewhat confused about his predicament.

The sultan began: "You have broken the law of the land with your brazen dishonesty. It was I to whom you so graciously fed sweets and tea while you told a string of lies." The sultan continued, "You said you were only twenty years old, but the kingdom's records show that you are seventy; you told us you have just a single son, but the records prove you have six; and finally, you declared your value to be only seventy-thousand *dinars* while the court records show that you are by far the second richest man in the kingdom." The sultan glared at his counselors and judge. "We need to show the people we are serious about our new law by jailing this man and fining him the maximum penalties.

The merchant looked surprised at these accusations, but not shaken. "Your majesty," said the merchant, "may I reply to these charges?"

The sultan, quite certain of himself, and impatient to mete out the first punishment, reluctantly nodded yes.

"By Allah, I have told you nothing but the truth. You asked me my age and I answered that I have had twenty good years—that is because my first twenty years were my happiest."

"You asked how many children I have and I answered that I have only one praiseworthy son: a single son who loves Allah and lives by God's laws. All my other sons are drunks who contribute nothing to the welfare of others." The merchant bowed his head in shame.

"And lastly, you asked me of my wealth. I replied that for Allah's sake I had saved seventy thousand *dinars*. Seventy thousand is the amount of money I paid to have the town mosque built—where people come to worship and where the poor are fed. I have no true real wealth but what I've given to others." The merchant stood humbly before the court, letting his words take their effect.

At last the sultan spoke up gently, with an apology, "The merchant is right of course." The sultan looked at the other men. "There is no time more happily remembered than when our spirit is full of love; there is no child closer to our hearts than the child who acts honorably; and there is nothing of value on this earth which is not done for God's sake."

A man came to the Prophet
Muhammad 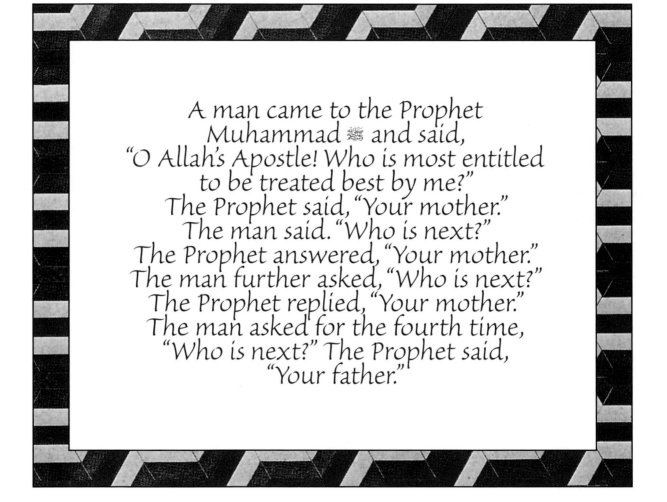 and said,
"O Allah's Apostle! Who is most entitled
to be treated best by me?"
The Prophet said, "Your mother."
The man said. "Who is next?"
The Prophet answered, "Your mother."
The man further asked, "Who is next?"
The Prophet replied, "Your mother."
The man asked for the fourth time,
"Who is next?" The Prophet said,
"Your father."

Whose Crown? A Tale from the Middle East

 Kan ya ma kan: there was and there was not a wise king who ruled over his people with justice and kindness. In order to encourage the people to contribute to the good of everyone, he decided to present a gold crown to the person who had served his fellow humans best.

At last the field of contenders was down to the final three, a poet, an artist and a scientist. A large group gathered at the palace to see which of the three would receive the golden crown. The king himself was to be the judge.

The poet went first, reciting his best-known poem which made the crowd sigh with pleasure. While the king was listening to the poem, his glance fell on an old woman at the front of the crowd. As the poet continued, she nodded her head slightly with a smile on her face which seemed to say, *Yes, this is the person who deserves the crown.*

Then it was the artist's turn and he displayed his most beautiful paintings. While the crowd oo'd and aww'd over the pictures, the king found himself looking for the old woman's reaction. To his slight surprise, she was again nodding and smiling at the artist, as if to say, *Yes, he is definitely the person who deserves the crown.* As for the king, he couldn't choose between the two.

The third contender was a scientist, presenting a collection of papers he had written in which he had made new advances in knowledge. The king found himself again looking at the old woman. She nodded and smiled, as if this third person was the very one that most deserved the prize. *If I took her advice, I'd have to award three crowns,* laughed the king to himself.

The king was having trouble deciding among the three. "Is there anyone else who would like to be considered for the golden crown?" he asked the crowd while he was thinking about the three men. "How about you, respected mother, have you come as a contender for the award?" he addressed the old lady with due honor for her age.

She stepped forward shyly, and answered, "The three men who stand before you today are all my sons, and I am here only to support them and see who will win."

At last the king knew which person had done the most good for others. He picked up the crown, descended from his throne and placed the crown on the head of the mother of the three men, saying, "Here is the person who has done the best. She has raised three children to be a credit and a goodness for us all."

Life has no meaning for him
who does not help
to make the world prosper more
than it did before,
or to give it happiness,
so that its bliss may grow.

Zah! A Tale from Iran

Once upon a time, there lived a king who took immense delight in gardens. One day, strolling along the roads of the city, admiring the various flowers and fruits tended by its citizens, the king came upon a poor, ancient gardener. Having newly cleared a small plot from some underbrush, the old gardener readied a pear sapling for planting.

"*Salam alaikum*, peace be with you," said the king. "I fear you are too old to work in the garden during the heat of day." The gardener had been so absorbed in loosening the sapling's root ball that the king's comments took him by surprise. He looked up.

"And besides," continued the king, standing over the gardener, "why bother to plant something you won't get to see grow in your lifetime? Any day now, you may sleep the long sleep of death."

The old gardener looked wistful, then replied, "Well, if I don't get to see it grow, I don't mind. Many will delight in its sweet fruit; others will enjoy the shade it provides from the hot sun."

154

"Zah!" exclaimed the king, using a Persian expression of joy. He smiled. "That is a very wise thing you have said." He then promised to reward the man with ten thousand *dirhams*.

"You see," said the old gardener with a twinkle in his eye, "My tree is already bearing fruit! Usually a tree requires many years, but my sapling has begun right away!" he chuckled.

"Zah!" exclaimed the king again with a large grin. "You have once more shown great understanding!" He crossed his arms and contemplated the distant hills briefly. "If I follow your advice in all my affairs, my kingdom will surely prosper for generations to come." And the king promised the old gardener yet another ten thousand *dirhams* as a prize for this insight.

The gardener stood up, thanked the king for both rewards, and clasped the king's hands within his own. "You see," said the gardener, "Ordinarily, trees only bear fruit once a year, but mine has already provided for me twice this season!" The gardener smiled a wide, toothless grin for the king and went back to his gardening.

"Zah!" said the king.

Haste is from the devil.

The Hidden Teacher: A Story of Malik Dinar

 After many years of studying philosophy and wisdom, Malik Dinar felt ready to see the world and learn from it on foot. Most of all, he felt curious about the inner, hidden teacher which he had read so much about. So one day, Dinar simply set off as any student might—with great enthusiasm, and in a hurry.

Not long into his first day, he crossed paths with a wise, old dervish named Fatih.

Said Dinar, "I am in search of the inner, hidden teacher. May I travel with you for awhile? Perhaps you can show me how to find it."

Old Fatih, used to this kind of request, agreed to let Dinar join him. Not two minutes into the journey Dinar then asked, "What can you teach me?"

The old dervish replied in the typical, puzzling way of dervishes, "What can *I* teach *you*?" he mimicked. "What can *you* teach *me* is more the point!"

Dinar, confused, said no more and Fatih kept quiet as well. They walked along in the afternoon heat until they approached a certain date palm tree.

"Wait!" said Fatih, stopping in front of the tree. He leaned into it and put his ear against the trunk. "This tree tells me, 'Oh, I hurt so! There is something in my side which stings. Will you please remove it?'"

Dinar guffawed. "Trees do not speak," he said, looking doubtfully at the old dervish. "And besides, we don't have time to take something out of its side. Look here, I am in a great hurry to meet my inner teacher, and we need to keep moving ahead."

"Suit yourself," said Fatih. He gave the tree a soft pat on the trunk and followed Dinar down the road. "I was only reporting what the tree told me."

Half an hour later Fatih stopped. "You know," he said. "I'm pretty sure I smelt honey around that tree. Maybe we should go back and collect some for our dinner."

"Of course!" Dinar agreed. "Honey is a rare find in these parts. If we decide not to eat it, surely someone will buy it from us in exchange for supper." So the two backtracked down the road towards the date palm. When they spotted the tree, they saw it was now surrounded by a small group of men.

"What's all this about?" asked Dinar when they got close.

"This tree," replied one of the men, "has enough honey in it to feed a city." He smiled. "My brothers and I are now honey merchants, *al hamdu lil Allah*, thanks be to God." The brothers turned from Dinar and Fatih and continued collecting the honey in pots. Dinar, sullen with this missed opportunity, started back down the road, Fatih in tow.

The next day, as they walked by a rocky mound right beside the road, Fatih halted. "Dinar," he said, "something is talking to me. I think it's the ants." Dinar stopped and looked at the dervish with a skeptical eye. "Yes," continued Fatih, "It *is* the ants! They are telling me, 'We are in the midst of a large excavation. We have worked and worked. But now we have run into some obstacles in our path. Have mercy! Please stop and dig out these obstacles.'"

Dinar shook his head slowly from side to side. "Fatih. How can ants talk to you? They are silent creatures. We don't have time for this nonsense! We can't dig up a mountain! Come, come, we must move on. I must find my inner, hidden teacher."

"As you wish," replied Fatih, following in step behind Dinar. "But the wise ones say that all things are connected," said Fatih. "These ants may well have a connection to us..." his voice trailed off as Dinar hurried away.

When they camped that evening, Dinar couldn't find his knife. Thinking that he might have dropped it on the road, he decided to retrace his route the next morning. The dervish came along. Approaching the rocky mound, they spotted a group of men sitting atop a pile of dirt and gold coins.

"What!" cried Dinar. "How did you know to dig here?"

One of the men replied, "An old dervish on the road told us to dig in this spot. He said, 'What is dirt to some is gold to others.'" The man grinned. "Actually, the dervish looked a lot like that old man with you!"

Fatih cut in, "Oh, all old dervishes look the same. Who knows where that dervish is?"

Dinar cursed as they walked away, "Why have I been so unlucky? That's twice! If we had stopped either time we would be rich."

The dervish mumbled a reply that Dinar, in a hurry, paid no attention to.

They continued traveling, and a few days later arrived at the bank of a beautiful, wide river. Across on the other side they spotted a ferryman, and waved for him to approach. While waiting for the boat, they witnessed an odd thing: a fish bobbed out of the water again and again, looking at them. "That fish," said Fatih at last, pointing to it in the water, "is seeking our help. The fish says, 'I need a certain herb on the bank there because I have something stuck in my stomach. It needs to come out. Have mercy on me and get me that herb!'"

Dinar, not as sure of himself anymore, thought about it. Perhaps this dervish could talk to creatures and maybe things are interconnected but … just then the boatman arrived. Dinar in his haste, pushed the dervish into the boat and then climbed aboard, happy to be moving again instead of wallowing in these confusing questions. Reaching the far shore, the two men spent the night at a tea house and no more was said about the fish.

The boatman woke them the following morning, kissing the dervish's hand and praising him for the luck the two travelers had brought him. Dinar rubbed his eyes, waking to the story. "You see," said the boatman, "although I was tired when you waved me over, I decided to come get you for the *baraka*, the blessings that come from helping travelers. When I at last docked my boat that night, I noticed a fish that had jumped out of the water, flopping towards a certain plant on the shore. I plucked the plant and gave it to the fish. Much to my surprise, the fish swallowed the herb and immediately coughed out a huge stone from its belly." By this time

Dinar was wide awake, fairly certain he had missed yet another remarkable opportunity. The boatman continued, "When I rubbed the stone clean, I saw it was a huge, flawless, diamond!" He wept and kissed the dervish's hand again.

"Aiee!" cried Dinar. "What kind of companion are you? You've known about these treasures all along and let me walk right by them!" Dinar stood up and stomped around the room. "I had no idea I was missing so much! Now misery will be my constant companion; I was better off before!"

As soon as Dinar spoke these words, he felt as if a great boulder rolled right through his soul, and he knew that exactly the opposite was true, and what he had voiced was a lie.

The dervish Fatih, whose name means 'the beginning,' touched Dinar on his shoulder, saying, "Now, brother, perhaps you will not be in such a hurry. You will finally be able to learn from experience: that is the true meaning of the inner, hidden teacher."

A few minutes later, Dinar watched the old dervish, Fatih, walking down the road. He was already surrounded by a new group of travelers, each of them arguing with the other, and each asking the Dervish about the journey before them.

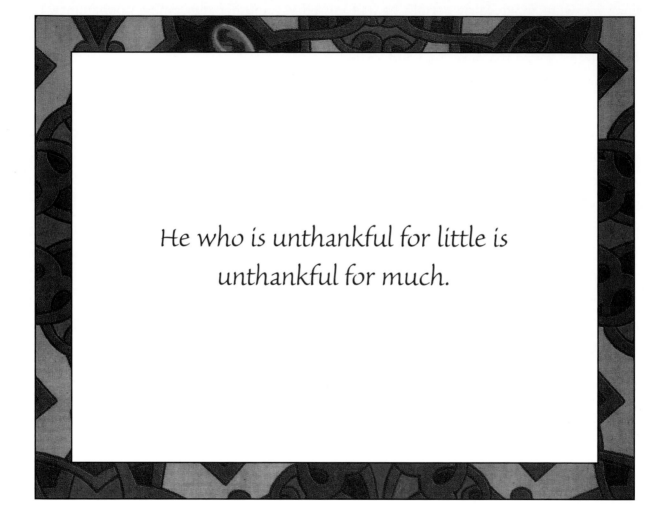

He who is unthankful for little is unthankful for much.

The Honorable Joha, Mulla Nasruddin Hodja, Goha Gives Thanks

 Kan ya ma kan: there was and there was not a time when Goha lost his beloved donkey. As Goha paced the streets of the town and ambled through the countryside in search of it, he praised God, "*Al hamdu lil Allah*! Thanks be to Allah! Thanks be to Allah for my lost donkey!" rang his cheery voice from the streets and fields.

Finally, one of the townsfolk stopped him: "Goha, why would you thank God for a lost donkey?"

Goha smiled, "If I had been riding that donkey, I, too, would now be lost. Thanks be to God it is only my donkey unable to find his way home!"

Notes and Sources

Holy Qur'an

Allah has revealed the most beautiful message,
A Book consistent in its verses
Yet repeating its teachings in different ways.
We have cited for mankind every kind of parable in this Qur'an
So that they might learn a lesson.
Qur'an 39:23, 27

"The beginning of the Divine Inspiration to Allah's Prophet was in the form of good dreams which came true like bright daylight," narrated Aisha bint Abu Bakr[1], his second wife. Those dreams were followed by revelations given to Prophet Muhammad ﷺ over a period of 23 years. The word, 'Qur'an' means 'recitation.' *The Holy Qur'an* is, word for word, the complete collection of God's words recited to the Prophet Muhammad by the angel Gabriel, which the Prophet in turn recited to people.

Many revelations came to address a particular situation that the Muslims were in at that time, but they continue to be relevant. For example, some of the first revelations stressed the oneness of God and the importance of doing away with idol worship. Idol worship can also refer to wealth and power which tempt people to worship something other than Allah.

[1] Sahih Al Bukhari vol. I, number 3

After belief in one God was firmly held in the hearts of believers, the Qu'ran revealed the other main elements of the religion: prayer, fasting, zakat (a particular form of charity) and pilgrimage. These are the five pillars of Islam, the first of which is belief in the absolute unity and oneness of God.

The Qur'an is a book of guidance and good ethics. And with each piece of advice comes the reminder that *Allah*—the Arabic word for God—knows all, and is the best judge of your deeds. When the Prophet Muhammad and the community of Muslims moved from Mecca, where they had been a persecuted minority, to Madinah, where they were welcomed, the revelations increasingly dealt with issues of governing and society. Ruling justly, being fair in business transactions, dealing kindly with your spouse and neighbors, and helping the old, the sick and the poor were some of the subjects of the revelations.

The Qur'an also contains stories of prophets who came before Muhammad, such as Ibrahim (Abraham), Musa (Moses), and Isa (Jesus), peace be upon them all. The Qur'an says in Chapter 16, verse 44:

We sent those prophets with clear signs and scriptures;
and now We have sent down the reminder to you,
so that you (O Muhammad), may explain clearly to mankind
as to what was sent to them so that they may think about it.

As each revelation was given to the Prophet Muhammad, he recited it to others and had at least one person write it down. Paper was uncommon at the time, so pieces of leather, palm fronds and other flat materials were used. The written revelations were collected in the order dictated by the Angel Gabriel to the Prophet. Before his death, the entire Qur'an was recited by him several times and repeated to him by many Muslims.

A few years after the death of the Prophet, vowel markings were added to prevent any mispronunciation or misreading, and official copies of the Qur'an were sent to the four corners of the Muslim realm. Today, 1400 years later, one of those copies can be found in the main library in Moscow, Russia, and another copy can be found in the Topkapi Museum in Istanbul, Turkey. If you compare one of those 1400-year-old Qur'ans with a Qur'an purchased in a store near you, you will find that they are exactly the same Arabic, word for word, and letter for letter. No matter where Muslims are located, whether in China or California, and no matter their local language, they all read the Qur'an in it's original Arabic.

Hadiths

For Muslims the Prophet Muhammad ﷺ was the living example of what was revealed in the Qur'an. Therefore his actions and his words are of supreme importance. Recognizing this, people around the Prophet were careful to memorize his actions and exact words. These actions and utterances are known as the *Hadith* of the Prophet. Some of them were written down at the time they happened, but many were related orally from one generation to another.

About one hundred years after the Prophet's death, Muslim scholars began to collect these hadiths and form them into collections. The most famous of these scholars is known as Al Bukhari, which is actually not his name, but the name of the place he was from, Bukhara, in central Asia. As with the other scholars, he was meticulous about his method of collecting hadiths. Each narrator of a hadith was scrutinized for his or her memory, truthfulness, and lack of bias.

Al Bukhari traveled all over the Muslim realm gathering these hadiths, and wherever he found one that he had also collected from another area, he compared the two to see if they were word for word the same. It is said that he once traveled a great distance to gather the hadiths of a certain person known to have memorized many. He found the man in a field with his horses. Trying to convince one horse to come to him, the man pretended to offer the horse some food. As soon as Al Bukhari saw this, he turned and started walking away. "Wait", said the man, "Don't you want to hear the hadiths that I know?"

"No," answered Al Bukhari, "A man who can lie to a horse, cannot be trusted to relate a hadith."

In this book, where we have written, "Narrated by such and such a person," that is the name of the person who saw the Prophet say or do the action, and who told others about it. A hadith is considered reliable and true if it has an unbroken chain of trustworthy narrators from the original witness to the collector.

Origins of the Honorable Joha, Mulla Nasruddin Hodja, the Folk Character

People around the Muslim world enjoy stories of the funny but wise Joha and his donkey. The first time Joha was mentioned in written form was in a line by a famous Arab poet, Umar ibn Abi Rabiyah, who lived around 700 CE.

The probable history of Joha is that he started as an Arab folk character, and then moved along with Islam to Persia, where his name changed to Mulla Nasruddin. Persian Muslim influence spread over a wide area, including India and Central Asia and the beloved Mulla Nasruddin won his place in the literary culture of all those regions.

Islam spread to China by way of the Silk Road and so did the Honorable Affanti, a.k.a. Joha, Mulla Nasruddin Hodja. Affanti, say the Chinese, was born in a certain province of China (the word 'affendi' is an honorary title in Turkish), and he rode on his donkey as far east as Xian and as far north as Mongolia.

When the Turkic people of Anatolia (present day Turkey) became Muslims, it seems they also adopted Joha, whom they called Nasreddin Hodja. The name Nasreddin is more correctly written as *nasr–Al–din*, which in Arabic means, 'Helper of the Faith.' The term Hodja is an honorary title denoting a scholar, in particular one learned in the Qur'an and Islamic law. To signify his special status as a scholar, a Hodja was allowed to wear a turban; thus, many of the stories feature Joha's turban.

Some Turkish people claim that Nasruddin Hodja was a real person who lived in Ak-Shehir near Konya in the Asian part of Turkey. Some say he was born in the 10th century, CE. Other stories are told of him dealing with Salahuddin in the 13th century, and still others have him standing up to Timur Leng (Timur 'the Lame') in the early 15th century. Many Egyptians and others also believe he was a real person who was born and lived in their own countries.

Not only has the Honorable Joha, Mulla Nasruddin Hodja become part of the culture in almost every Muslim land, his character and his stories have been adopted and adapted in Western European literature: some may recognize Joha's influence in *Don Quixote* and even in the oldest French book, *Fables of Marie de France.*

How do we know that the Affanti of China is the same folk character as Goha in Egypt? Sometimes the same story is told in both places; sometimes an unmistakable element of a Joha story appears in a different costume and setting in lands far apart. As far as we know, only our Honorable Joha, Mullah Nasruddin Hodja, uses his donkey's tail to help him get out of rough spots.

Name	Country
Joha	most Arabic speaking countries
Goha	a few Arabic speaking countries with a different dialect
Mulla Nasruddin	Iran, Pakistan, India, Kashmir, Azerbaijan
Nasruddin Hodja	Turkey, Bosnia, Greece
Koja Nasreddin	Kazakhistan
Mushfiqi	Tajikistan
Affanti	China
Abu Nuwaz	Tanzania

Sources of Quotes and Sayings

The Honorable Joha, Mulla Nasruddin Hodja and the Famous Donkey Story
"Life: sometimes the man on the saddle, sometimes the saddle on the man." *Caravan of Dreams* (traditional proverb), by Idries Shah.

The Bandage: A True Story of Rabiah Al Adawiya of Basra
"While you still have the power of speech use it in gladness and joy! Tomorrow, when the Angel of Death appears you will have no other choice than silence." *Sayings from The Rose Garden/Gulistan by Saadi*, translated by Omar Ali-Shah.

The Brothers: A Hausa Tale from West Africa
"God brings forth the living from the dead,/ and brings forth the dead from the living;/ and God enlivens the earth after its death:/ and so will you all be brought forth." *Qur'an:* Sura 30 (The Romans), ayat 19.

It's Not the Sun: From the Qur'an
"There is no compulsion in religion. /True direction is in fact distinct from error: /so whoever disbelieves in idols and believes in God/ has taken hold of the most reliable handle which does not break." *Qur'an:* Sura 2 (The Heifer), ayat 256.

Manifold Increase: A True Story of Uthman ibn Affan

"The human race is created from the one source. If one man feels pain, the others, from the same source, cannot be indifferent to it." *Sayings from The Rose Garden/Gulistan by Saadi*, translated by Omar Ali-Shah.

The Honorable Joha, Mulla Nasruddin Hodja and the Tricky Case

"How can one obtain wisdom?" asked a boy. Mullah Nasruddin replied, "Always listen attentively to what the wise and learned men tell you. And if you are speaking to others, listen carefully to what you are saying." *202 Jokes of Nasreddin Hodja*, Minyatur Yayinlari.

The Wise Sailimai: A Tale from China

"The true work is in the heart." *Sufi Women, Revised Second Edition: Rabiah*, by Dr. Javad Nurbakhsh.

All in the Family: A Tale from Pakistan

"Avoid Suspicion as much as possible: for suspicion in some cases is a sin: and spy not on each other nor speak ill of each other behind your backs." *Qur'an* 49:12.

What if? A Tale from Iran

"Eat your bread in such a way / that the bread / does not become your master." *The Hundred Tales of Wisdom: Life, Teachings and Miracles of Jalaludin Rumi from Aflaki's Munaqib*, by Idries Shah.

The Honorable Joha, Mulla Nasruddin Hodja and the Pumpkin Tree

"And God knows what is on the land and in the sea; / and not a single leaf falls but God knows it." *Qur'an* 6:59

Words to Live by: A Tale from Iran

"The cure of ignorance is to ask and learn." Hadith from *Sunan of Abu Dawood, # 146.*

Hajar and Ismael: From Hadith

"Worship God as if you see Him, and remember that even if you see Him not, He still sees you." Hadith from *Sahih Al Bukhari*, vol. I, #47.

The Castle in Cordoba: A True Story of King Hakim

"If you want to sleep at peace beneath the ground, make tranquil the hearts of beings above it." *Perfume of the Desert* (Sayings by Saadi), translated by Andrew Harvey and Eryk Hanut.

The Honorable Joha, Mulla Nasruddin Hodja, Affanti and the Donkey's Tail

"Good deeds are a shining light." *Four Centuries of Swahili Verse*, Verse 5, trans. by Jan Knappert.

True Inheritance: a Tale from Iraq

"Nobody has eaten better food than that won by his own labor." Hadith from *Sahih Al Bukhari*, vol. 3, #286.

A Tent for the Emperor: A Tale from Turkey

"Success will follow patience, / Opening will follow hardship, / And ease will follow difficulties." Hadith, *Essential Sufism*, by James Fadiman and Robert Frager.

The Parrot and the Grocer: A Tale from Iran

"The strongest among you is the one who controls his anger." Hadith from *Sahih Al Bukhari Vol 8, # 135* .

The Head and the Lute: A True Story of Bayazid Bustami

"True servants of God are those who walk humbly on the earth and say: "Peace!" to the ignorant who accost them." *Qur'an 25:63*.

The Clever Kantchil: A Tale from Indonesia

"What is wisdom? Do what you should do when you should do it. Refuse to do what you should not do; and, when it is not clear, wait until you are sure." Hadith, *Essential Sufism*, by James Fadiman and Robert Frager.

The Best Investment: a True Story of Rabia ar Ray

"Knowledge is better than wealth. Knowledge guards you, while you have to guard wealth. Wealth decreases by spending, while knowledge multiplies by spending." *Nahjul Balagha* by Ali ibn Abu Talib.

The Price of a Secret: A Tale from Azerbaijan

"Nothing on earth is so deserving of a long imprisonment as the tongue." *Arabian Wisdom* by John Wortabet.

The Honorable Joha, Mulla Nasruddin Hodja Feeds His Coat

"Surely God does not judge you by appearance or property but by the goodness of your heart and deeds." Hadith, *Essential Sufism*, by James Fadiman and Robert Frager.

Know Yourself: A Tale from the Middle East

"Give now of your gold and wealth, for soon it will pass from your grasp. Open the door of your treasure today, for tomorrow the key will not be in your hands." *Perfume of the Desert* (Sayings by Saadi), trans. by Andrew Harvey and Eryk Hanut.

Infant Jesus: From the Qur'an

"Surely Allah is with those who are patient." *Qur'an* 2:153.

What the Birds Know: A Tale from Iran

"Do they not observe the birds above them/spreading their wings and folding them? None/could hold them except the Compassionate Allah; surely it is He Who watches over all things." *Qur'an* 67:19.

The Water Pot and the Thief: A True Story of Rabiah Al Adawiya of Basra

"If you would be rich, choose only contentment, for it is the only true richness." *Sayings from The Rose Garden/Gulistan by Saadi*, translated by Omar Ali-Shah.

The Storm: A Tale from Iran

"Plan for your life as if you will live forever/Work for the Hereafter as if you will die tomorrow." Well known saying of Ali ibn Abu Talib.

Trustworthy Traveler: A True Story of Abdul Qadir Jilani

"Truth brings peace to the heart." *Arabian Wisdom* by John Wortabet.

The First Supporter: A True Story of Khadija bint Khuwailid from Hadith

"And among His Signs is this, that He created for you mates from among yourselves that ye may dwell in tranquillity with them and He has put love and mercy between your hearts; verily in that are Signs for those who reflect." *Qur'an* 30:21

It Is So: A Tale from Mali

"God exalts the humble and humbles the proud." Hadith, *Essential Sufism* by James Fadiman and Robert Frager.

Gate of Knowledge: A True Story of Ali ibn Abu Talib

"Stars are the beauty of the heavens, and learned men are the ornament of a people." *Arabian Wisdom* by John Wortabet.

The Best Witness: From Hadith

"Trust in God, but tie your camel." Hadith, from *Essential Sufism* by James Fadiman and Robert Frager

The Honorable Joha, Mulla Nasruddin Hodja and the Judge

"Stand out firmly for justice and bear true witness for the sake of God even if it against yourselves." *Qur'an* 4: 135

The Web and the Dove: from Hadith

"A man is not alone, /is not alone,/he has God, /he is not alone." *Four Centuries of Swahili Verse*, Verse 7, trans. by Jan Knappert.

True Worth: A Tale from Syria

"Not everything that is great in size is great in value." *Sayings from The Rose Garden/Gulistan* by Saadi.

Whose Crown? A Tale from the Middle East

"A man came to Prophet Muhammad ﷺ and said, 'O Allah's Apostle! Who is most entitled to be treated with the best companionship by me?' The Prophet said, 'Your mother.' The man said. 'Who is next?' The Prophet answered, 'Your mother.' The man further asked, 'Who is next?' The Prophet replied, 'Your mother.' The man asked for the fourth time, 'Who is next?' The Prophet answered, 'Your father.'" Hadith from *Sahih Al Bukhari*, vol 8, #22.

Zah! A Tale from Iran

"Life has no meaning for him who does not help/to make the world prosper more than it did before,/or to give it happiness, so that its bliss may grow" From *Four Centuries of Swahili Verse*, verse 10, trans. by Jan Knappert.

The Hidden Teacher: A Story of Malik Dinar

"Haste is from the devil." Proverb, *Caravan of Dreams*, by Idries Shah.

The Honorable Joha, Mulla Nasruddin Hodja, Goha Gives Thanks

"He who is unthankful for little is unthankful for much." From *Arabian Wisdom*. John Wortabet.

Story Sources

To the Reader

The life of the Prophet Muhammad ﷺ can be found in many biographies, and in hundreds of hadiths. The sources of these stories are *Sahih Al Bukhari*, vol. 3, #551, and vol. 8, #26. The verses from the Qur'an can be found in Surah 17:9.

The Honorable Joha, Mulla Nasruddin Hodja and the Famous Donkey Story

According to the people of the Arabian Peninsula, the Honorable folk character of Joha was a man who was born and who is buried on that peninsula. I (F.C.) first heard this story from an Egyptian many years ago, but I've heard it again and again, from Turks and Moroccans, Iraqis and Iranians. I used this story to find the name of Joha in a particular country. "Do you know any stories of Joha?" I would ask. "No, I don't think so," they might answer. "Have you ever heard about the man who carried his donkey on his back?" I would persevere. "Oh, yes, we know that story. It's about a man called ...." and I would hear the name I was looking for, Mulla Nasruddin in Pakistan or Affanti in China.

The people in the Arab world love Joha so much and tell so many stories about him that you might think that he must belong exclusively to them. That is, until you visit Iran.

The Bandage: A True Story of Rabiah Al Adawiya of Basra

Rabiah Al Adawiya was born in Basra (in present day Iraq) in 713 CE. She dedicated her life to praying to God, and is famous for her religious steadfastness, refusing marriage, wealth and fame as they were offered to her. Her poetry is well known among Arabic speakers, and many stories are told of her. The story of the bandage can be found in *Sufi Women* by Javad Nurbakhsh.

The Brothers: A Hausa Tale from West Africa

This tale of life and death is told by the Hausa people who, according to their oral history, became Muslim in about 635 CE. They were originally organized in city-states, but are now mostly in northern Nigeria. Two good sources of their stories are *A Treasury of African Folklore*, collected by Harold Courlander, and *Hausa Tales and Traditions*, in three volumes, translated and edited by Neil Skinner.

It's Not the Sun: From the Qur'an

The Qur'an is a book of guidance which contains many stories used to illustrate its truths. There are several about the Prophet Ibrahim (Abraham) who is revered by Muslims as well as by Jews and Christians. The original story, written in Arabic, is beautifully written. Unfortunately when it is translated, the writing becomes stilted. We have tried to remain true to the stories from the *Qur'an* and hadiths, while presenting them in a more readable fashion. This story stresses that there is only one God, which is the central message of Islam, and the first of its five pillars. Abraham's story is in *Qur'an*: Surah 21, *(The Prophets)*, ayat (verses) 51-71 (ayat means 'signs' in Arabic and is used in the Qur'an as English uses the word 'verses'), and in Surah 6: (The Cattle) 76-79.

Manifold Increase: A True Story of Uthman ibn Affan

Uthman ibn Affan was one of the first people to accept Islam. A very wealthy merchant known for his honesty and integrity, he put all this wealth in the service of the early Muslim community in Madinah. There are many stories of how he shared his wealth, and this is perhaps the most famous of them. He later was chosen, by consensus, to be the third Caliph, or leader, of the Muslim realm. This story can be found in *Anecdotes from Islam* by M. Ebrahim Khan; *More True Stories for Children*, translated by Matina Wali Muhammad; and *Heroes of Islam* by Mahmoud Esma'il Sieny.

The Honorable Joha, Mulla Nasruddin Hodja and the Tricky Case

According to the people of Iran, Mullah Nasruddin was either a real person born in Persia, or their own national folk character. Not only do the people tell stories about him for the pleasure of laughter, but his stories are often used to illustrate important and paradoxical truths. This story shows how important it is for a person to practice what he preaches. It is found in *The Pleasantries of the Incredible Mulla Nasrudin* by Idries Shah. The people here love Mullah Nasruddin so much that you might think that he belongs only to them. That is, until you visit Pakistan.

The Wise Sailimai: A Tale from China

Islam in China spread by conversions and by intermarriage with non-Muslims, mainly along the Silk Road, and along the coast. In relation to the total number of Chinese people, Muslims are a small minority. However because China is by far the most populous country in the world, that small minority represents perhaps as many as 60 million people. That means there are more Muslims in China than in any country in the Middle East. The Muslims in China are known as Hui people. *Mythology and Folklore of the Hui, a Muslim Chinese People* collected by Shujiang Li and Karl W. Luckert is an excellent source of their cultural heritage in which this story can also be found.

All in the Family: A Tale from Pakistan

This story shows exactly how important it is for us to work together, each using our unique talents for the good of all. The idea of consulting together for the good of everyone, *shurah* in Arabic, is an important principle in Islam. The parts should have thought about what was best for themselves *and* for the stomach, in order to take care of everyone's needs. This tale is found in *Golden Tales 3* by Akhlaq Husain.

What if? A Tale from Iran

This story is taken from *Kalila wa Dimna,* a collection of animal fables and shrewd commentary on political life. The original tales were translated into old Persian from the Indian fables of Bidpai, and then translated again into Arabic in 750 CE by Ibn Al-Muqaffa in what is considered the oldest work of Arabic prose. 400 years later it was translated into modern Persian. Over the years, stories have been added and dropped but the collection flourishes. Although this story is not an animal tale, it is told by an animal to illustrate a certain point. It is found in *Kalilah and Dimnah: Stories for Young Adults*, translated from Persian and adapted by Muhammad Nur Abdus Salam.

The Honorable Joha, Mulla Nasruddin Hodja and the Pumpkin Tree

According to the people of Pakistan, Kashmir and India (who share much of the same culture) Mullah Nasruddin is a famous folk character of their countries. He has the same name as his Persian counterpart due to the influence of Persian culture on that area when it was part of the Muslim realm. This story, using pumpkins, is found in *Folktales from India* by A.K. Ramanujan. The same story using watermelons instead of pumpkins is in *Watermelons, Walnuts and the Wisdom of Allah: A Collection of Turkish Stories* by Barbara Walker. The people in these countries love Mullah Nasruddin so much that you might think that he was a real person from that area. That is, until you visit China.

Words to Live by: A Tale from Iran

This story was written by one of the most famous Muslim writers, Farid al Din Abu Hamid, from Nishapur (in modern Iran) around 1200 CE. He is known by his pen name 'Attar'. This and other stories can be found in *Attar: Stories for Young Adults*, translated and adapted from the Persian by Muhammad Nur Abdus Salam.

This story was also told by the 19th century poet Asrar Sabzevari in verse: A king had a valuable pearl to set in a ring;/ All of his rings had gemstones./ He wanted an inscription with a double meaning/ (To remind him) whenever he looked at it:/ That he not be negligent when he was rejoicing,/ That he not suffer unduly when he sorrowed./ He approached the wise of his age,/ But found their suggestions unsatisfying;/ At that juncture, a dervish appeared/ And said: "Write these words: 'This Too Shall Pass.'"

Hajar and Ismael: From Hadith

Many times the Prophet Muhammad ﷺ told stories to illustrate Qur'anic truths. Arabs trace their lineage (ancestry) back to Ibrahim, through his son Ismael, born of Ibrahim's wife, *Hajar*; Jews trace their lineage to Abraham through his son Isaac, born of Abraham's wife, Sarah.

When the Prophet Muhammad told the story of Ibrahim and *Hajar*, he interrupted the story to point out that not only did *Hajar* have complete trust in God, but she also did whatever she could to help herself and her child. This story is found in *Sahih Al Bukhari*, vol. 4, number 583 and 584. The prayer of Ibrahim is found in the Qur'an in Chapter 14, "Ibrahim", verse 37 and was quoted by Prophet Muhammad while telling the story.

The Castle in Cordoba: A True Story of King Hakim

Al Hakim was the Amir, or King of Andalus (Muslim Spain) from 796-822 CE Among his accomplishments was an extension of the Grand Mosque of Cordoba and the establishment of the first university in Europe, also in Cordoba. This true story can be found in many sources in Arabic, and several in English, including *Anecdotes from Islam* by M. Ebrahim Khan, *Folk-lore of the Holy Land* compiled by J.E. Hanauer and *Short Stories of Islamic history* by C.T. Dutt.

The Honorable Joha, Mulla Nasruddin Hodja, Affanti and the Donkey's Tail

According to the people of China, the Honorable folk character is named Affanti. They are quick to tell you that he was born in a certain province of China, and is as Chinese as they are. I (F.C.) found this in a small book of stories, written in Chinese, in a bookstore in Beijing. I can't read Chinese but I recognized my friend at once because the cover illustration showed a man riding backward on a donkey —a Joha story found in many countries. When I asked our guide if he recognized the character, he said, "Oh, yes, of course. Everyone knows about Affanti." The name 'Affanti' doesn't sound Chinese, but it is very similar to the Turkish word, 'Affendi' which means 'Sir'. My friend Mariam Wang translated the version told in this book. Variations of this story are found in *Tales of the Hodja* by Charles Downing, and *The Incredible Mulla Nasrudin* by Idris Shah. The Chinese love him so much that you may think that he really was a person who spent his life there. That is, until you visit Turkey.

True Inheritance: A Tale from Iraq

This story, about the value of hard work and honest labor, was first told by Hasan of Basra (in modern Iraq) in the 700's. Five hundred years later Roger Bacon used it as a teaching story at Oxford, England. Five hundred years after that it was claimed by the seventeenth century chemist Boerhaave. Today you can find it in *Tales of the Dervishes* by Idries Shah.

A Tent for the Emperor: A Tale from Turkey

There are several versions of this story, some of which are also well know in Greek folklore. The version cited here is attributed to Sheikh Mohamed Jamaludin of Adrianople, (in modern Turkey), who lived in the early 1700's. It can be found in *Tales of the Dervishes* by Idries Shah.

The Parrot and the Grocer: A Tale from Iran

This is one of Jalaluddin Rumi's teaching tales. He is one of the most celebrated and most widely translated Sufi teachers of all times. Interestingly, he is also the most widely read/recited poet in both the United States and Afghanistan. The original story of the grocer, the parrot and the dervish focuses more on the dervish's advice (to the parrot) that nothing causes more blunders than the habit of judging things by their appearances—such as a bald head. We chose to focus on the grocer's unchecked anger, however, and its unforeseen consequences. It can be found in *Tales from the Land of the Sufis*, "Jalaluddin Rumi" by Mojdeh Bayat and Mohammad Ali Jamnia.

The Head and the Lute: A True Story of Bayazid Bustami

Bayazid Bustami was a famous Sufi scholar and teacher who came from Bustam (in modern Iran). He lived from 746-877 CE In this story he exemplifies how best to respond to those who attack you either verbally or physically. Many stories about him can be found in *Tazkeratul Aulia* by Attar and *Anecdotes from Islam* by M. Ebrahim Khan.

The Clever Kantchil: A Tale from Indonesia

According to Islam, God created everything—including all animals—and all animals (except humans) are created obedient to Allah. Therefore, when the crocodiles hear what sounds like a command from God, they are quick to obey. This tale can be found in *Kantchil's Lime Pit and Other Stories from Indonesia*, by Harold Courlander.

The Best Investment: A True Story of Rabia ar Ray

Rabia ar Ray was a great scholar and teacher in the early 700's. His students included Imam Malik bin Anas, after whom the Maliki school of law is named, and Hasan al Basri, a leading scholar of Qur'anic explanation (*tafsir*). I (F.C.) heard this story many years ago but needed the details as related by Samer Bondock, an Egyptian friend. A slightly different version can be found in A Mother's Rights, by Matina W. Muhammad, translator.

The Price of a Secret: A Tale from Azerbaijan

The unhealthy consequences of secrets and gossip are addressed often in Islam. This story was told by Hakim Nizami of Ganje, a leading Persian medieval epic poet. He is especially renowned for his two romantic tales, *Layla and Majnun*, and *Khusrau and Shirin*. He was born between 1155 and 1162, in Azerbaijan. He was reportedly well versed in all the sciences of his time, such as mathematics, Islamic law, Greek philosophy and medicine. This story is from "The Great Secret of Alexander," *Tales from the Land of the Sufis*, by Mojdeh Bayat and Mohammad Ali Jamnia.

The Honorable Joha, Mulla Nasruddin Hodja Feeds His Coat

For one month every year, Muslims fast from before the sun rises, until it has set. Fasting is another of the five pillars of Islam. Therefore Nasruddin Hodja has not had any food or water since before the sun rose. Unlike meals at other times, the Ramadan dinner is not delayed if guests are late, so he has a difficult choice to make.

According to the people of Turkey, the Honorable folk character Nasruddin Hoja was born in the town of Horto, Turkey in the year 1208; others say he was born there, but much earlier or much later I first heard this story from an Egyptian. It is also No. 131 of *202 Jokes of Nasreddin Hodja, by Yazinlari, Istanbul*. Another version of it is found in *Arab Folktales*, translated and edited by Inea Bushnaq who attributes it to Syria.

Know Yourself: A Tale from the Middle East

Generosity is the most well known quality of Arabs. As you can see, no one in the story is suggesting that the man should not be generous, but the question is, just how generous should he be? The man had already paid the *zakaat*, charity, that he owed (the third pillar of Islam is *zakaat*, about 2.5% of one's excess wealth due every year), so the excess he gave the woman came from knowing his own sense of fairness. This story can be found in *Stories from the Arab Past*, by Denys Johnson-Davies.

Infant Jesus: From the Qur'an

This is one of several stories about Jesus in the Holy *Qur'an*. This story is found in Surah 19, "Mariam:" (Mary in English) 16-34. Jesus is respected and revered by Muslims as one of the special people that God appointed as prophets to mankind. According to the *Qur'an*, Jesus was born of a virgin birth, and he performed many miracles. Allah clouded the eyes of the soldiers who came to arrest Jesus, and raised Jesus into heaven. The *Qur'an* also points out that it was as easy for Allah to produce Jesus from one parent as it was for Him to make Adam without any parents.

What the Birds Know: A Tale from Iran

Here is another story from that famous collection, *Kalila wa Dimna*. Danadil was on his way to the *Ka'bah* in Mecca (in present day Saudi Arabia) when the robbers attacked him. Making a pilgrimage, *hajj* in Arabic, to the *Ka'bah*, the first house of worship to God, is required once in the lifetime of every Muslim who is able. It is one of the five pillars or tenets of Islam. One of the *Hajj* rituals is to run back and forth from the hills of Safa to Marwa as *Hajar* did when she was searching for help. The story of Danadil can be found in *Kalilah and Dimnah: Stories for Young Adults*, translated and adapted by Muhammad Nur Abdus Salam.

The Water Pot and the Thief: A True Story of Rabiah Al Adawiya

Rabiah Al Adawiya is also known as Rabiah of Basra, the place she was born. Regular prayer five times a day is one of the pillars, or basic teachings of Islam. The physical part of the prayer involves standing, bowing, and kneeling with your forehead touching the ground. The prayer includes praise and thanks to Allah, as well as requests for help and guidance. This story can be found in *Sufi Women* by Javad Nurbakhsh.

The Storm: A Tale from Iran

In an earlier story, "The Head and the Lute" you were introduced to Bayazid Bustami, a famous scholar and teacher who came from Bustam (in modern Iran). "The Storm" is one of the stories that he told. It can be found in *Tales of the Dervishes* by Idries Shah. Although mankind has free will and can choose much of what happens, death is one thing people have no control over. According to Islam, Allah decides when and where one will die. Since we don't know when that will be, we should always try to do our best, so we are ready whenever it happens.

Trustworthy Traveler: A True Story of Abdul Qadir Jilani

Abdul Qadir Abu Swaleh, known as Abdul Qadir Jilani for his birthplace, Jilan, in present day Iran, was born in 1052. He is one of the most respected Sufis and scholars of Islam. This story is found in many sources, including *Stories Good and True* Matina Wali Muhammad, translator, and *Hundred Great Muslims* by K. J. Ahmad.

The First Supporter: A True Story of Khadija bint Khuwailid from Hadith

Khadija bint Khuwailid was a strong, wealthy, independent woman who lived in Mecca (in present Saudi Arabia) at the time of Prophet Muhammad ﷺ. Not only is she remembered as the wife of the Prophet, but she is honored for her good character, courage, honesty and generosity. The common practice in the days before Islam was for a man to consider his wife as his property and to have many wives, perhaps eight or more. When Islam came it freed women, asking them to keep their own name, and specifying that any wealth the wife brings to the marriage and all that she gains in the marriage belong solely to her. Khadija therefore kept her wealth when she married the Prophet, and it was totally her decision as to how it should be spent. Islam did not forbid plural marriages, but limited the number to a maximum of four wives.

In the first part of the story, the angel Gabriel appeared to Prophet Muhammad as an enormous figure which covered the horizons. According to Islam, at other times angels appear as normal humans, as they did with Mary and with *Hajar,* (other stories in this book). This story is taken from the hadiths in *Sahih Al Bukhari*: Vol. 1, number 3; Vol. 4; number 605, and Vol. 6, number 468.

It is So: A Tale from Mali

Seidu has a double dose of undesirable pride. First, he is proud to be brave, when he is, in fact, a coward. Second, even if he had been brave, he should not have been proud because according to Islam, it is God who gives us our special qualities. Therefore, we have nothing to be proud about, and in fact we should be humble and grateful for our talents and blessings.

This story also demonstrates how people in a close knit community like the Hausa gently correct each other's faults, and then forgive and forget the problem. *A Treasury of African Folklore* by Harold Courlander contains this and other stories from the Muslim peoples of Africa.

Gate of Knowledge: A True Story of Ali ibn Abu Talib

Imam Ali was the closest male relative of the Prophet ﷺ. He was known for his courage as well as his scholarship, his generosity as well as his wisdom, his ability to judge as well as his ability to rule with humility. Upon the death of the Prophet the community had to decide how to choose the next leader. The majority felt that the best qualified person was Abu Bakr and they gave him their allegiance. A few at that time, and larger numbers later on, felt that Ali should have succeeded his cousin due to his lineage. This was the cause of the split which resulted in Shi'as who wanted Ali, and the majority Sunni who chose Abu Bakr. Among the books containing stories about him are: *The First Intellectual Muslim Thinker: Imam Ali ibn Abi Talib,* by Muhammed Abdul Rauf; *Anecdotes from Islam* by M. Ebrahim Khan; *Heroes of Islam* by Mahmoud Sieny; and *Nahjul Balagha: Peak of Eloquence: Sermons, Letters and Sayings of Imam Ali ibn Abu Talib,* trans. Sayed Ali Reza.

The modern biography with its close attention to historical accuracy was developed by Muslims as they sought to record the exact events of the time of Prophet Muhammad. They wrote accurate biographies of many of the people who were with him, known as the Companions of the Prophet, which included Imam Ali. These biographies have throughout the ages and throughout the Muslim world been passed down from grandparents as sources of guidance and wisdom.

The Best Witness: from Hadith

This story was told by Prophet Muhammad ﷺ to illustrate how important it is to keep your promise, and how you can depend on Allah to help you, if you do everything that you can. Before the time of Prophet Muhammad, no one named themselves Muslim. Therefore when Prophet Muhammad told of earlier people who followed the teachings of the one god, Allah, he told it about Jews and/or Christians.

Lending and borrowing money is acceptable in Islam, but only as a business partnership—without interest. If the merchant made a profit, he would return more than the original amount he borrowed.

If he had lost his cargo, he would not return the money at all since the lender is a partner in the business. The story is found in *Sahih Al Bukhari*, vol. 3, number 488B. It is retold in many children's books, including *The Story of 1000 Dinars* by Umar and Salimah Salim.

The Honorable Joha, Mulla Nasruddin Hodja and the Judge

According to the people of Turkey, the Honorable folk character Nasruddin Hodja is buried near the town of Aksehir, Turkey. You can see for yourself the place where they say he is buried. There is a huge gate with an enormous lock on it, but don't worry. If you want to get inside, just walk around the gate as there is no fence on either side! There are many stories in Muslim lore that emphasize how important justice is, and the importance of judges being of admirable character. This story is found in *202 Jokes of Nasreddin Hodja* by Minyatur Yayinlari, Istanbul Turkey. The Turkish people love him so much that you may think that he really belongs to them exclusively. That is, until you visit Egypt.

The Web and the Dove: A Story From Hadith

This story is found in biographies of the Prophet, including *Sirat Rasul Allah* by Ibn Ishaq in about 700 CE, translated by A. Guillaume, as *The Life of Muhammad*, and *The Life of Muhammad* by Muhammad Husayn Haykal, translated by Isma'il Al Faruqi.

True Worth: A Tale from Syria

Real truth is not always obvious. On one level the man appears to be telling lies, but on closer examination it turns out that he was talking about a higher truth. This story can be found in *Arab Folktales* by Inea Bushnaq, and *The Cow of No Color: Riddle Stories and Justice Tales from Around the World*.

Whose Crown? A Tale from the Middle East

The family is the basis of Islamic society, and the mother is the most important although everyone has an important role. Many stories relate how children should respect their parents, and other stories, such as this one, point out the importance of the mother. This story can be found in *Stories from the Arab Past* by Denys Johnson-Davies.

Zah! A Tale from Iran

It is important to do what is good for others, even if you will never benefit from it. An Arab proverb states: "Others sowed for me; I sow for others to come." This story can be found in *A Mother's Rights* by Matina Muhammad.

The Hidden Teacher: A Story of Malik Dinar

As with many Sufi stories, this one is meant to be interpreted on several levels: story, parable, and allegory. Was there really an old dervish who showed Malik Dinar the way or did Dinar realize that he was, in his haste, simply missing the spiritual treasures surrounding him everyday? Malik Dinar was one of the early classical Sufis. This version of the story is told by Emir El-Arifin, "The Initiation of Malik Dinar" in *Tales of the Dervishes* by Idries Shah.

The Honorable Joha, Mulla Nasruddin Hodja, Goha Gives Thanks

According to the people of Egypt, the Honorable folk character is named Goha. They are quick to tell you that he is the national folk character of their country or that he was definitely born in Egypt. This particular story can be found in *Goha*, by Denys Johnson-Davies, Hoopoe Books, and *The Fabulous Adventures of Nasruddin Hoja*.

The Egyptians love him so much that you may think that he really was an Egyptian. However, a book bought in Egypt, titled *Goha and His Anecdotes*, by Farouk Saad, Lebanon, says that he first appeared as Joha in the Arabian Peninsula. So now we have circled around the globe and are back to our original introduction to Joha. He is not so much a national folk character as he is a member of the world-wide Muslim community.

Acknowledgements

First, my heart-felt gratitude to the dynamic and talented trio at Eastern Washington University Press— Chris Howell, Scott Poole, and Joelean Copeland—who have given me the encouragement and support to pursue this series on world religions for youth. I would also like to acknowledge Valerie Wahl, the illustrator of the series, for the magic she brings to these pages. Finally, I am grateful to my co-author, Dr. Freda Crane, for her flexibility, great passion for the book's purpose, exactitude and a willingness to persevere.
—Sarah Conover

Foremost my thanks to Sarah for insisting that I co-author this book with her. I would also like to thank everyone in my family: my husband Mohammed, my children Riyad and Noura, my son-in-law Yassir Syeed, and my daughters-in-law Mollie Brewsaugh and Rana Barazi who helped in both accuracy of information and editing. I would also like to thank my daughter Karima, and my sons Rasheed and Samir, for taking care of the grandchildren so the rest of us could work on the book. Thanks also to friends who contributed and or translated stories and quotes: Mariam Wang, Samer Bondok, and Omar Tarazi. A special thanks to my almost-family friend Goha, who introduced me to a world-wide culture many years ago.
—Freda Crane

About the authors

Sarah Conover has long-standing interests in world religions and education. She holds a BA in Religious Studies from the University of Colorado and an MFA in Creative Writing from Eastern Washington University. Her first book, *Kindness: a Treasury of Buddhist Wisdom and Stories for Children*, published by Eastern Washington University Press in 2001, won the Skipping Stones Award for Cultural Diversity and was chosen by ALA's *Booklist* as one of the ten best spiritual books for children in 2002. Her second book, *Daughters of the Desert: Stories of Remarkable Women from the Christian, Jewish and Muslim Traditions*, which she co-authored, was published by SkyLight Paths Press in May, 2003. She lives with her husband Doug Robnett, and her two children, Nate and Jamey, in Spokane, Washington. She teaches humanities at a public high school, where she tries to interest students in solving the world's problems. This is Sarah's third book.

Freda Crane is an educator who has worked on developing Islamic curriculum on three continents. She received her MA in Curriculum from the University of California, Berkeley, and her EdD from the University of Cincinnati in Ohio. She has traveled widely collecting Muslim literature from as far away as China, and as close as the nearest used book store. Dr. Crane has been a Muslim for over thirty years, teaching and developing instruction for Islamic schools in the United States, Saudi Arabia, South Africa, and Malaysia. She was the children's book editor for American Trust Publications, an Islamic publishing company, for several years, and has long been active in the educational activities of the Islamic Society of North America.

Dr. Crane currently lives in Cincinnati, Ohio, with her husband Dr. Mohammed Shamma. They have five children and five grandchildren, one of whom is named Ayah Jamilah, "Beautiful Sign." She is in charge of curriculum development at FADEL, the Foundation for the Advancement and Development of Education and Learning.

About the illustrator

Valerie Wahl currently lives in Spokane, Washington, and works at The Northwest Museum of Arts and Culture. She has read thousands of books to her children but this is her first try at illustrating a series. *Kindness, A Treasury of Buddhist Wisdom for Children and Parents,* is the first in EWU Press' *This Little Light of Mine Series. Ayat Jamilah: Beautiful Signs,* is the second book in the series. She is a graduate of Washington State University where she studied Fine Art.